BAYOU ROSE

NIGHTGARDEN SAGA #4

LUCY HOLDEN

FEHU PRESS

For Emma and Kate
Whom I love with all my heart
- Aunty P.

THE NIGHTGARDEN SAGA

Book #1: Red Magnolia
Book #2: Moonvine
Book #3: Poison Berry
Book #4: Bayou Rose
Book #5: Dusky Dahlia
Book #6: Blue Lilies
Book #7: Night Shade

There is also a prequel, told from Antoine's perspective, available on my website. Go to www.paulaconstant.com to download.

PROLOGUE

ear Tessa,

Connor and Cass remain in the bayou. I know Connor comes here during the day. I see the work he has done, his tools where he left them. But he waits until I am at school to arrive and is gone when I get home. Once I came home early, just to try to catch him, but our brother is a wolf now. He was gone before I parked under the magnolia.

Antoine goes quiet when I ask about Connor. He's tried to reason with him, I'm guessing. I could have told him it wouldn't work. The brother we knew is gone now, lost in his wolf's body and his love for Cass. I wish I could simply let him go as easily as it seems he has me. But I miss him. I miss them both. Connor is all that is left of us, Tessa, of the family we once were together. Losing him feels like someone cut a part of me away without anesthetic. Antoine does his best to fill that space, but even he cannot take the pain away, though I love him so much that I sometimes feel guilty—for being so happy when you are dead, and Connor is gone.

It's all so confusing.

Antoine makes me go to school. I know Mom wanted us to get our high school diplomas, and to honor her memory I'm doing my best to complete senior year, but I think we all knew I was never the college type. Without Cass, and with Keziah's shadow lurking just out of sight, school feels as cold as the mansion does with no Connor inside it. Even Avery is more distant. She spends more time with Remy than with me, now, and there seems to be a hard edge to her voice sometimes when she talks about Connor. I think his leadership of the wolves has caused some problems, though she doesn't tell me anything, and at times I feel like she blames me for all of it. We aren't friends in the same way we were before all of this.

Jeremiah and I have become increasingly close at school. He spends as much time at the mansion as he does at the house he and Antoine supposedly share, though Antoine hasn't spent a night there in weeks now.

I'd be lying if I said that last sentence didn't make my stomach flip a little. But I can almost see you rolling your eyes at me, so I won't talk about the nights. I'm not sure I'd have the words, anyhow.

Antoine and I don't talk about my so-called powers, whatever they are. It's the one subject that we both stay away from. So do Tate and Jeremiah. I figure that's Antoine's doing. I know he's worried. If I'm honest, Tessa, I'm worried too, and not just for myself.

Antoine doesn't say anything, but I suspect Keziah is calling him again. He seems so grim sometimes, like there's a battle going on inside him. At first I thought it was only my imagination. Then Avery let something slip in class one day that made me think Cass is struggling, too. Keziah is still out there, waiting, preying on us all. It's like we're living in the interval between acts in a play, waiting for the curtain to go up and show us the next scene.

It's an uneasy interlude.

I've filled it by starting a water garden. I know you probably think I should just stop growing anything, but I can't help it. Planting is the only thing that helps the loneliness go away. The night garden is riotous and full, but since Connor became a wolf, I can't bear being in it. The water garden is sunlit joy, a peaceful little pond just above a curve of the river, where I have planted bulbs of lilies and lotus. They're still hiding beneath the murky surface, but when they bloom, they should come up as a beautiful sea of light yellow and blue, like a reflection of the sun and sky.

I feel as if we all need as much sunlight and joy as I can create.

I'm writing this down on the jetty. I painted today: a lotus, just like those I've planted. It made me feel warm inside. It's the first painting I've done in forever, and I'm actually proud of it. I think I will hang it in my bedroom, to remind me that even when I feel like winter will never leave my heart, there is always sunshine, somewhere. No matter how dark and tough he is, I think our brother needs that sunlight too. He needs us, Tessa. Maybe even more than we ever needed him. But I don't know how to bridge the gap.

I love you so much, Tessa. I'm glad I buried your ashes here. I feel you, in the whisper of wind and the soft, slow movement of the river. I know you are always with me.

If you have any power over there, wherever you are, I hope you are whispering to Connor, too.

Your twin,
Harper

CHAPTER 1

SPRING

$\mathcal{I}$t's late afternoon on a Sunday, and puff clouds drift across a dreamy spring sky. The river is moving slowly, and I'm knee-deep in it, feeling for the water lily and lotus bulbs in the rich silt below. The scent of wildflowers mixes with apricot on a soft breeze, and for a time at least, I can forget that my brother is no longer family, and that a vampire who wants me dead is still on the loose.

"You look like a hobo."

I smile without turning around. "Gardening is hardly a fashion event."

"Gardening." I can hear the amusement in Antoine's voice. It makes my stomach curl in a slow, warm feeling. "In a hat that is more brim than anything else, a pair of shorts barely worthy of the name, and a bikini top? You should definitely garden more often."

"And boots," I say in my defense.

"Let us not forget the boots." I turn around to find him leaning against the red magnolia that hangs over the water garden, arms folded, regarding me with hooded eyes and a lazy smile that makes my pulse race. I know that look.

"I probably smell like river water," I say, backing away. But he's fast, too fast, and before I finish speaking, he has lifted me up and placed me on the red magnolia branch, one hand resting on the base of my spine, the other splayed on the trunk beside me.

"I don't know." He leans in so his lips are at the soft part behind my jaw. "You smell like springtime," he murmurs, and then my arms are around his neck and for the next while, even my lotus bulbs are forgotten.

"We should go in," I whisper a while later. "It's getting cool out."

"Is that right?" he gathers me closer. "I hadn't noticed."

"Dinner," I begin weakly.

"Can be ordered in."

"Jeremiah—"

"Is at the river house."

He kisses me again, and it's hard to so much as think, let alone speak, and I vaguely wonder why I am arguing. Just as I'm giving in to the idea that dinner might end up being pizza, I feel him tense against me. He turns to look out over the river, and in the golden sunlight full of bugs and river haze, his eyes are steel grey and somehow distant, as if he's gone somewhere I can't follow.

"Antoine?" I say uncertainly. His arms are still around me, but the warm intimacy of moments ago is gone, replaced by cold detachment. "Antoine?" I repeat, more concerned this time. A moment later he turns back to me, his eyes snapping into focus, as if he's just remembered where he is.

"Dinner." His voice is strained, and the smile he gives me doesn't reach his eyes. "Maybe we should have something healthy, after all." He gives me the same forced smile and lifts me easily off the branch, carefully brushing the scraps of bark from my legs, but managing to avoid my eyes.

"What's wrong?" I ask bluntly.

"Nothing. I think a cloud passed over the sun. You're right—it's getting cool out." He turns away and starts collecting my gardening tools. I stare at his back, but he doesn't offer anything more, and I let it go, for now.

A while later I've washed the river off, night has fallen, and Antoine is grilling steaks on the porch while I toss a salad. Despite all the work Connor has done on the mansion, the makeshift kitchen that opens onto the front porch is still where we spend most of our time. I know it will be renovated soon, returned to the parlor it once was, but it's the only room in the mansion other than my bedroom that really feels like home. If I'm honest, it also feels like Connor, and when I'm here, it's as if he still is, too, in the comforting remnants of our old existence —the beer stein I once gave him on top of the icebox that I've kept even though we have a refrigerator now, and his tools lying about on the shelf.

"He'll find his way back, in time." I turn to find Antoine watching me, his eyes dark. I know he worries about Connor and me. He knows how much I love my brother. Right now, though, Connor isn't the one on my mind, for once.

"What happened earlier?" I'm directly facing him, so I see the opaque veil that falls over his eyes as I ask the question. "It's her, isn't it," I say when he doesn't answer. "Keziah."

His arms are folded and he's leaning against the doorframe, the steaks lying forgotten on a plate on the sideboard. There is a faint crease between his brows, and he looks away evasively. "I can tell." I try and fail to find his eyes. "I remember how it was, with Cass and Avery."

"It isn't the same." His response is clipped and hard, but it doesn't deter me.

"If she's trying to get into your head, there is a way we can make sure we keep her out."

The crease between his brows deepens in momentary confusion. Then his eyes widen, and he almost shudders with distaste as he realizes what I'm suggesting. "I told you once before that I'd never drink your blood again," he says curtly. "I meant it, Harper. Don't ever suggest that. Don't even think it."

"Why not?" I fold my own arms and lean against the table, glaring at him. "It's the one thing we know works. Until we find a way to . . . end her, it might be the only way to keep you safe." I can't quite bring myself to say the word *kill*. Is it really killing, when the creature is Keziah, an ancient being that is something even more dead—and deadly—than a vampire?

Antoine opens his mouth for what I know is going to be a fierce rejoinder but, seeing my face, sighs and rubs a large hand over his face and around the back of his neck. "I know you mean well." I can tell how hard it is for him to keep an even tone. "But you can't begin to imagine how repugnant I find the thought of using you to fight Keziah. Of taking your blood as my own shield." He meets my eyes, cavernous darkness in his own. "Can you understand that?"

"I understand that you are proud." I step forward and put my hands on his face. "That you don't want to admit weakness. But have you considered that you might be the only one who can protect me? What happens if you don't take my blood, and Keziah gets into your head?"

For a moment I see shadows shift in the darkness, and I think it's worked, that he will listen to me. Then he covers my hands with his own and shakes his head, smiling ruefully as he brings our clasped hands down between us. "Good try," he says wryly. "You almost had me there."

"It's true," I insist, but I know the moment has passed.

"Harper." He puts his arms around me so they rest loosely at the base of my spine. "If I start drinking from you—where does it stop? *When* does it stop? And what if it is hurting you some-how, or binding you to me in a way that could be used against you?" He shakes his head. "Whatever runs through your veins, it isn't normal human blood. It's something so potent it contains the force of the earth, of water. It's magical." He smiles crookedly. "But when it's in my system, it's also all I can think about. And right now, I don't want to think about your blood, Harper. I just want to be with you." He pulls me closer, his lips hot and disturbing against mine. "I want to be with you so much I can barely think of anything else," he murmurs, and now my arms are about his neck, and when he pushes the steaks to one side and lifts me onto the sideboard, food is the last thing on my mind. "I won't drink from you," he says against my mouth, his hands twining in my hair. "But I will protect you, Harper. I swear it. If you believe nothing else—believe that."

And then there is nothing but heat and the wild night, and dinner winds up as cold steak and salad, a long time later.

CHAPTER 2

STORMS

For all that Antoine denies it, Keziah's calls weigh him down. He spends more time at the river house, making the excuse that I need to focus on studying for finals, which are barely weeks away. He shies away from any mention of Keziah's name.

Keziah herself doesn't come to school anymore, a small mercy for which I should probably be grateful, but instead makes me uneasy. Without regular contact with the wolves, I'm unsure of her whereabouts, though occasional rumors of increased death rates in the small bayou settlements do reach Deepwater from time to time. I wish I could ask Remy or Avery. But Remy and the wolves are in the bayou with my brother, as lost to me as he is. Avery spends all her available time with Remy. Going by the way he almost consumes her when he collects her in the parking lot from school, there is clearly no confusion about their relationship anymore. I feel sorry for Jeremiah. He never says anything, but I see him watching Avery with Remy, and I know it must hurt. I think he misses her friendship as much as anything else. I know how he feels. With

Cass in the bayou cabin with Connor, and Avery immersing herself in Natchez law with Remy and his mom, Lori, it's just Jeremiah and me.

"Have you noticed anything off about Antoine lately?" Jeremiah asks me abruptly one morning as we are walking toward class. The sky shimmers with May heat and the aftermath of an overnight storm. Summer is almost here, school almost over. I've already submitted my artwork. These last weeks feel like the calm before real life begins, whatever that looks like for me.

I take my time before I answer him. "Like what?" I say, careful to keep a neutral tone. Jeremiah stops just beyond the school doors and faces me.

"Last night I couldn't sleep," he says. "I came downstairs to get a drink, and Antoine was standing at the glass doors that face onto the river. They were all open wide, even though it was a windy night, with lightning in the sky."

"He likes storms," I say unconvincingly. "Especially the summer electrical ones."

"We all like watching the summer storms, Harper," snaps Jeremiah. "But we don't generally stand still as a statue while rain pounds in through open doors."

I suppress a faint shudder. There is something about the image his words conjure up that makes me feel as if the storm is still here, all around me. "So what is it that you're trying to say?" I know my question sounds defensive, but I also don't have answers.

"I think Keziah is calling him again." Jeremiah shoots me an almost apologetic glance.

"She is," I say flatly.

"You already knew?"

"I knew." I try to smile at him. "We talked about it."

"If Keziah is calling him, don't you think we should be doing a little more than talking about it? What if he can't fight her off?"

"I know, Jeremiah, okay?" I interrupt his indignant flow. The steps have almost cleared, and we're about to be late for class. "Antoine says he can handle it. And he won't accept what help I can offer."

"You mean—" Jeremiah looks around and lowers his voice. "Your blood?"

"Yes, my blood." I meet his eyes. "Antoine won't drink it."

"Why not?"

"Because," says a third voice which makes us both spin around, "Antoine has always fought his battles alone." Tate has materialized at our side. With his long hair tied back, wearing jeans and a faded plaid shirt, he looks less the history teacher he is impersonating and more like an ad for an outdoor magazine. "Taking Harper's blood would be admitting weakness. It would go against every moral code to which Antoine has ever held himself."

"Moral codes won't help any if he winds up Keziah's slave again," says Jeremiah, clearly unmoved by this argument.

"Isn't there something you can do?" I ask Tate. "It's getting worse, I can tell. And he won't talk to me about it."

"He won't speak to me, either." Tate gives me a resigned look. "Although I'm not sure why I thought he would, given he hasn't confided in me for the past three centuries." He walks past us into school. "Since you're supposed to be in my history class," he says over his shoulder, "you should probably come too."

"Why are you still pretending to be a teacher, anyhow?" Jeremiah mutters to Tate as we go inside. "Keziah's not coming to class anymore."

"She could return at any time. Not a chance Antoine or I am prepared to take. And besides," Tate casts us a wry smile, "I enjoy it more than I thought I would."

In fact, Tate is a wonderful teacher. He's so much more engaging than Mr. Larkin, whom he compelled out of the job in winter term, that I know for a fact the school board has already offered him a large raise to stay. I suspect Tate is considering taking it, too. He seems to have slotted into Deepwater life with the diplomacy that is his vampiric gift, charming the women of the Historical and Legacy Societies, enchanting his students, and making himself so helpful to other staff members that even the most conservative and single of the female teachers bat their eyes when he wishes them good morning.

Today the students look up eagerly as he pushes open the classroom door. They are crowded around a tablet which Jared Baudelaire waves eagerly in Tate's direction as we enter. "Mr. Garrison," he says excitedly. "We found something about the tribe in Haiti we were reading about last week."

"The Taíno?" Tate puts his bag down on his desk. His head is down. There's something in his voice, a certain tension, that goes unnoticed by Jared, but makes Jeremiah and I exchange a wary glance.

"Yes, them." Jared points at the tablet. "Apparently, there was a god or something called Macocael, who was supposed to stand guard over a mountain cave during the day. When he left his post, he was punished by being turned to stone. The Taíno worshipped him as a god. They had really cool symbols, called zemis, that they used to represent their gods."

"An impressive, if somewhat sketchy, summary of a very complex indigenous culture," Tate says. He's smiling, but an odd shadow lurks at the back of his eyes, and instead of drawing the conversation out as he normally would, he turns it to a discussion about the impact of colonial settlement on indigenous cultures. The class is interesting, but I notice he steers away from any conversation about the Taíno culture. By the end of the class, Jared seems to have forgotten anything about it.

"This is our last class," says Tate as we are packing up. Everyone pauses and stares at him.

"Why?" Jared is frowning. "We're barely weeks from our final exam. You can't just leave."

"Mr. Larkin will be here to answer any questions you might have." He holds up a hand as a general groan rises from the class. "And I will also be available by phone and email. But to be honest"—he smiles around warmly—"you've all worked very hard, and I think you can look forward to very good results." Despite their desire to look cool, even Jared and the jocks seem appeased by that, going by the bashful looks and mock punches they throw at each other. I wonder if it's only Jeremiah and me who notice that Tate never answered Jared's question.

"So where are you going?" I ask under cover of everyone clattering their chairs.

"I have a project overseas." Tate is looking down at his bag and doesn't meet my eyes.

"To do with the Taíno, that tribe in Haiti?" Jeremiah comes to stand beside me. Tate still doesn't look at us.

"Will this project help Antoine?" I ask. That makes him look up.

"I don't know," he says quietly. "But it may help me understand Keziah. And if I understand her, perhaps, yes, I might find a way to help Antoine—and Cass."

"I thought you said you'd studied mythologies all over the world, researching her?" The room is empty but for the three of us now.

"I have." Tate slings the bag over his shoulder. "But it seems I was looking in the wrong place. Until last week, when our good friend Mr. Baudelaire stumbled across an internet article about the Taíno, and I did some more research." He meets my eyes. "You have to understand," he says with a faint smile, "the last time I researched Caribbean tribes, nobody was discussing the Taíno. Their culture had been hidden from white attention, thought long gone, if thought of at all. And at the time, I was focusing my attention on African cultures." He shrugs. "I just missed it," he says, and I can tell by the crease between his brows that he blames himself for the oversight.

"And now you think there might be some clues there?"

"Perhaps." His expression is guarded. "But you must understand, Harper: I've followed a hundred leads before. This is just as likely to produce nothing more than those did."

"But it might." I can hear the same excitement in Jeremiah's voice that I feel, a glimmer of light at the end of the dark, oppressive tunnel Keziah's existence has cast over our lives.

"It might," Tate concedes reluctantly, turning away. "I have to get to class."

"When are you going?" I call after him.

"I fly from Jackson tonight." The glance he gives me is guarded. "But don't get your hopes up, Harper. I've chased these rainbows before."

Despite Tate's reluctance to feed my optimism, the rest of the day passes in daydreams of a Keziah-free life, one where Antoine's face doesn't go dark and detached with an internal war he won't allow me to help him fight. When I emerge from school to find him waiting in the lot, I feel my heart surge in a way that not even Avery racing away from me with barely a backward glance or so much as a cursory greeting can diminish.

"You look happy." He gives me the twisted smile that always makes my stomach curl. He's leaning against his teal Chevy truck, impossibly handsome in an open linen shirt over faded jeans, showing just enough corded arm muscle that a nearby group of girls cast me an envious glance and erupt into nervous giggles when they pass.

"You shouldn't come to school." I smile as he pulls me close. "You are far too distracting to the student body."

"There's really only one student body I'm interested in," he murmurs, kissing me in a way that has even the conservative female teachers casting me glances of mingled envy and disapproval. He opens the door and I climb into the truck, aware of the curious eyes watching us. I know our relationship separates me from the rest of my class and draws the concern of teachers, many of whom have taken me aside at one time or another to inquire, in their caring but extremely clumsy manner, if I might need to speak to the school counselor. Since what I would have to say would end with me locked in an institution, I've waved off their concerns, but I know they talk about me behind the staff room door. Tate and I have laughed about it, more than once, even though I suspect Tate shares their concerns.

"You're in a good mood." I glance sideways at him as we drive out of town. "Jeremiah said you had a difficult night."

His face tenses. He reaches over and takes my hand, softening his face with a noticeable effort. "Jeremiah shouldn't concern himself."

"He knows what it is, Antoine. We both do. Even Tate knows." He lets go of my hand and stares out the window, his face set and hard once more. "There's no point being angry," I say impatiently. "We just want to help."

"And if I need help," he says tersely, "I will ask for it." I'm opening my mouth to argue when he slams the brakes on, bringing the truck to a sliding halt just beyond the mansion gates.

"What is it?" I peer through the thick branches of the live oak along the driveway.

"There's someone at the mansion." He cocks his head, every sense alert, then relaxes slightly. "Human. A girl, younger than you." He turns to me. "Are you expecting anyone?"

I shake my head. "Not that I know of."

He turns through the gates and we approach the house slowly. Antoine is right. Sitting on the steps is a thin girl with a pointed, pixie-like face and very short black hair. She has wary eyes and clutches a worn duffel bag close to her side as she watches me get out of the truck.

"Hi." I smile at her. "I'm Harper. Were you looking for me?"

"Kind of." She doesn't return my smile but stares instead at Antoine. "Is your name Connor?"

"No." Antoine isn't smiling either. "But perhaps you might like to tell us yours?"

"My name is Callie." The girl clutches her duffel bag protectively. "I'm looking for Connor Ellory. He's my brother."

CHAPTER 3

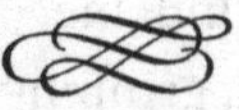

CALLIE

"*Y*our brother?" I stare at her.

"Sure." Callie speaks in a thick Memphis accent. "Gareth Lafayette is my daddy, though I didn't know nothin' 'bout that 'til my momma passed a month ago. Found my birth certificate, had his name on it. Found Gareth, too, after a time, but it seems he ain't much more use than my momma was." She shrugs. "They both liked the bottle. Probably why they was together. Only difference was, Momma moved on from the bottle to other things, which is why she ain't around no more."

She's such an odd mixture of tough and weird that I'm not entirely sure whether to laugh or be concerned. I feel oddly protective of her, especially at her next words. "Gareth told me he got a son—my brother—old enough to be a legal guardian." She meets my eyes defiantly. "I ain't lookin' for nothin'. Just a signature on some papers to stop me going into the system. Coulda forged them myself, truth told, but I'm doin' right by coming here before I do. Y'all don't need to see me again." She casts a skeptical look over her shoulder at the decaying ruins of the mansion. "I can see y'all don't got much, anyhow."

I can't help it. Despite my shock, my lips twitch into a reluctant smile. "Antoine," I say, "maybe you could leave us. I'll call you later, okay?"

"You sure?" But one look at Antoine's tightly pressed lips tells me he, too, is struggling not to grin.

"Oh, I'm fairly sure I can take it from here."

"You know where to find me." He touches my waist and opens the door of his truck, grinning openly now. "Nice to meet you, Callie."

"I don' know as we did, but sure." She shrugs and watches the truck pull away. "That your old man?"

"I suppose he is, yes."

"Tasty."

I ignore that. "Won't you come inside?"

She casts me a wary look. "I'll do just fine here."

I shrug. "Suit yourself." I go inside and get two sodas, bringing them back out onto the porch. I open them both and when Callie looks at her can suspiciously, place it beside her. "I promise it's not laced with anything," I say.

"Sure." She still doesn't pick it up.

"Connor doesn't go by the name Lafayette anymore," I tell her. "He changed it to Ellory, same as mine. Gareth was my mom's boyfriend for a time, too." I glance at her. "After yours, I guess, since you must be what, fifteen?"

"Then Gareth ain't your daddy?"

"No. Mine died when I was young."

"Your momma?"

"She died, too. A few years ago." I take a deep breath. May as well get it all over now. "I had one other sister, Tessa. She was my twin. She died as well. Almost two years ago now. Connor lived with us when we were kids, and Mom and Gareth were together. He stayed in touch, and when Mom got sick, he moved in with us and never left."

"That must have been nice for y'all." To my surprise, there's no bitterness in her voice. "I don't think he would have known 'bout me. Seems Gareth didn't, neither." She picks up the soda absentmindedly and drinks from it. "Took him a while to remember my momma's name. When he did, he weren't interested anyways. Told me 'bout Connor, but only after I bought him a bottle. Took most of it to get the address out of him."

"I'm surprised he had it. Connor doesn't really try to keep in touch." That is an understatement. Connor gave up hope of his father ever climbing out of a bottle a long time ago.

"So, he here, then? Connor?"

I try not to grimace. "Yes and no." Realizing how that sounds, I try to smile. "Connor does live around here," I say. "But he's got a new girlfriend now, and a lot of responsibilities. He does come by the mansion every day. Just not at this time."

"Oh." Callie's eyes, bright blue in the gamine face, are somehow older than her years. "The two of you don't get on, huh."

"It's complicated."

She nods sagely. "Well, you give me an address, I'm outta your way for good."

"I'm not sure that's such a good idea." I wince internally at the thought of Callie turning up at the bayou cabin, where a newborn vampire is spending most of her time hanging out with a pack of wolves. No, definitely not a good idea. "Why don't you stay here tonight? I'll call Connor, let him know what's happening."

She looks at me narrowly. "You ain't gonna call services? 'Cos if you are, I'll be gone before they catch me. Done it plenty of times before."

I feel a rush of sympathy. "I won't call them," I say quietly. "I promise. Nor will Connor. We've had plenty of experience staying out of the system, believe me. Nobody here will let them take you away, Callie. You have my word." She watches me shrewdly as I speak. When I finish, she stares at me for another moment, then gives a decisive nod. "Well, okay, then. But I'm not askin' for nothin'. So we're clear."

"Sure," I stifle another urge to laugh at her hood talk. Somehow it seems like an act, a role she pulls on for cover. Her eyes are sharp and intelligent, and one of the books peeping out of her bag is Hemingway's *The Sun Also Rises*. Hardly lightweight reading for a girl of fifteen. I suspect there is rather more to Callie Lafayette than her baggy trousers, army boots, ripped T-shirt, and hood accent suggest. "I'm cooking pasta for dinner, though, and I'm sure there's enough for two, if you'd like some?"

"Only if it ain't costin'."

"It's not. I make the pesto myself, and spaghetti is in my budget, I promise."

"Well, alright then. Though can't say I've ever eaten pest . . . whatever you call it."

"Pesto." I lead her inside. "And you'll like it, I think."

While Callie is taking a shower—the first hot water she's seen in a while, I suspect—I text Connor: *I need to see you. It's about Social.*

If there's one thing guaranteed to get Connor here, it's the threat of Social Services. We've had more than one run-in with them over the years since Mom died. The closest I've ever seen my brother come to outright violence was when one particularly self-righteous social worker threatened to take me away, shortly after Tessa died. I honestly thought Connor was going to bodily throw her out of our apartment. We'd left Baton Rouge before she could make good on her threat.

But that was the old Connor, I think to myself as I grind up the basil and pine nuts for the pesto. I've no idea how the new version is going to react.

Connor must have been working close by, because his truck pulls up outside while the water is still running upstairs. He appears in the door with the silent, lethal grace I'm yet to become accustomed to, and once again I'm struck by the changes in his physical body. Connor is unmistakeably taller, by at least five inches, and his body has a lean, hard fluidity it never did before. His eyes are dark and penetrating, his face remote. He's always been handsome, but now he is magnetic, with the same unnaturally perfect features it seems all supernatural beings are blessed with.

"What's happened?" he says abruptly, by way of greeting. "You said Social found us. How did that happen?"

"Not us." I wipe my hands on a dish towel and turn to face him. "A girl called Callie. Callie Lafayette." His eyes flare slightly at the name. "She's Gareth's daughter, Connor. Her mom died recently; I gather she was an even worse addict than your father. She found Gareth's name on her birth certificate and tracked him down. Gareth sent her here. To you."

After a short silence, Connor says, "There's no point in her being here."

I frown. "She has nowhere to go, Connor."

"Well, I don't see how that's my problem. Let Gareth deal with it."

I stare at him, dumbfounded. "We both know Gareth *won't* deal with it, Connor. He can't. That's why she's here."

"She's here because Gareth told her I've got money now." I'm so taken aback by this that I can't find words to respond. "I'm sorry, Harper, but we both know we're in no position to take someone else in, not with everything going on. What am I supposed to do—take her out to the bayou with Cass and me? Or were you planning to install her here, with you and Antoine?" He folds his arms and meets my eyes with a grim stare. "What were you going to tell her about the cellar, Harper? About your night garden—or that new thing you're making in the wetlands by the river?"

"Water garden," I say feebly. "It's a water garden."

He twists his mouth dismissively. "Whatever it is, it's hardly something you can explain to a long-lost relative. She's better off away from here, Harper. Away from us. Whatever she's come from can't be any worse than what she'll find here. And I've done my years of raising other people's kids."

His words hit my heart like poisoned arrows, so sharply tipped I can physically feel the pain. "Other people's kids?" I repeat hollowly, staring at him. "Is that all Tessa and I mean to you now, Connor? Do you really hate me that much?"

For a moment something passes behind his eyes, a hint of the brother I used to know, but it is fleeting, quickly replaced by the hard wolf who is a stranger. "I don't hate you, Harper," he says roughly. "But you aren't my responsibility anymore. Cass is. And there's no way she'll cope with this, on top of everything else. Certainly not some sister from a crack addict I don't even know. And if you'll take some advice—though going on past experience, you probably won't—I wouldn't let her stay with you, either. If she's anything like Gareth, all she'll bring is trouble."

The kitchen crackles with charged silence. Too late, I realize the water has stopped running upstairs. As I do, Connor is already turning toward the corridor, where a pale-faced Callie, clad in a threadbare T-shirt and old shorts that have definitely seen better days, is staring between us both. "Callie," I say, stretching out a hand, "I'm so sorry—Connor didn't mean—"

"Sure he did," she says, in a high, hard little voice. "Ain't no problem. Nobody need tell me nothin' twice. I'll get my bag."

She turns and disappears, and I round on Connor, who at least has the grace to look uncomfortable. "How could you?" I say fiercely. "After everything we've been through, how could you cast out your own blood without so much as a word of kindness?" When he doesn't answer, I point at the kitchen door. "Get out of my house," I say coldly. "It might be your project, but it's my home, and I will decide who lives under its roof. For what it's worth, that isn't you. Not anymore. Not after this." I shake my head as Connor stares at me, still and silent as if he's a statue. "Who are you?" I whisper. "I don't even know you anymore, Connor. Just go." I turn my back on him, heading upstairs after Callie. "Just go."

I don't turn back, and by the time I'm at the top of the stairs, I hear the sound of his engine, gunning angrily down the driveway.

CHAPTER 4

HUNTING

It takes most of the night to convince Callie she doesn't have to leave. Even so, I get up before dawn to check her room and am not overly surprised to find her bed empty, though it's clearly been slept in. I'm reaching for my phone when I see her duffel bag in the corner. So she's still here, then.

A movement from beyond the window catches my eye. Down on the jetty, by the river, a thin figure moves slowly in the growing dawn. With surprise I realize it's Callie, doing something that looks suspiciously like tai chi. She holds a long sword in her hand that gleams in the sun as it flickers before her. As I watch, she comes to stillness and bows to an invisible master. She slides the sword back into a worn leather sleeve that she zips up. A moment later, she has dropped to the boards and into a series of very energetic push-ups. I watch her long enough to feel uncomfortably aware of my own lack of fitness, moving away from the window before she notices me.

"There's cereal in the cupboard," I greet her when she pokes a cautious head through the kitchen door. She's drenched in sweat, and by my calculations has been working out for at least an hour, beyond whatever she did before I spotted her on the jetty. She holds the leather sleeve protectively close, but I pretend not to notice. Maybe I should be bothered about the sword, but somehow her movements with it seemed peaceful, an act of meditation rather than aggression.

Then again, I think somewhat resignedly, *maybe I just like deadly things.*

"Mind if I take another shower first? I won't bother you after that. There's a bus from the center of town—"

"Callie." I face her with coffee in hand. "You're staying. I told you last night. It doesn't matter what Connor said. This isn't his house, and it's not his decision. You'll stay here as long as you need or want to, and whatever papers need signing, you can leave in my hands. You won't have any problems, I promise you."

She gives me a suspicious look. "You're not much older than me. Social won't let you sign, ain't nohow."

"You remember Antoine, from yesterday?"

"Your ol' man."

"I'd rather you didn't call him that. But yes, in fact, he's my husband." I color as I say it, forcing my voice to remain steady. Callie's eyes drop to the emerald on my hand and widen. "Your husband," she repeats disbelievingly. "He give you that rock?"

"He did." Briefly Connor's warnings of theft cross my mind, and I push them away, but not before Callie's eyes narrow knowingly.

"You don't need to worry none. I ain't no thief. Besides, I got a little cash left from Memphis. An' I'll get a job soon enough, I always do." I'm about to protest that I don't need her money, but she's already heading upstairs for the shower.

We eat in reasonably peaceful silence. It's a Saturday, so there's no school. Just as we're finishing up and I'm wondering what to do with my new charge, Jeremiah's motorcycle roars up the driveway. He bursts into the kitchen, speaking through his helmet, clearly oblivious to Callie in the corner.

"It's getting ridiculous, Harper. You need to talk to him. Last night—" he breaks off as he catches sight of Callie. "Sorry." He colors. "I didn't realize you had someone here."

"This is Callie. Callie, Jeremiah. Callie is Connor's sister." I shoot Jeremiah a look that warns him not to ask any questions. "She's going to be staying with me."

"For how long?" Realizing how he sounds, Jeremiah tries to recover. "I mean, that is—"

"I'm starting to see why folks complain about family." Callie pushes her chair back and reaches for her duffel bag. "Full of secrets and weirdness, y'all are. Never mind. I won't bother you longer'n necessary, like I said. I've got an interview at the lumberyard at nine, so I'll see y'all some time." She's gone before I can protest, jogging down the driveway, duffel bouncing on her back.

"She's not going to run into town, is she?" Jeremiah looks after her doubtfully.

"It wouldn't surprise me," I say dryly, sipping my coffee. "She's not exactly the most normal kid I've ever met." I tell him the backstory as we tidy the dishes.

Jeremiah frowns. "But that's so unlike Connor."

"I know." I shrug. "I have to believe I'll get my brother back one day. But for now, all he seems to care about is Cass. And I don't even know how she is. I haven't so much as laid eyes on her since the night of the Midwinter Ball, when Keziah killed her mother." I shake my head. "Anyway. What was it you were saying when you arrived? About Antoine?"

Jeremiah leans against the bench, flicking the towel moodily. "He's getting worse, Harper," he says without preamble. "He's angry, all the time. Distant. He doesn't sleep, and he never eats. I mean, I know he doesn't need food, but he used to at least pretend, just to be sociable, you know? Now he's barely at home."

I frown. "Then where is he?" I know Antoine has an office at the river house, where he manages his financial holdings, which I gather are substantial. It helps, I imagine, having eternity to invest. He also has a large shed there where he restores the old vehicles he loves and tinkers with the boat he likes to take out fishing.

"He's been out hunting a lot. Not that kind of hunting," he says hastily, seeing my face freeze. I know Antoine drinks from humans. He usually goes far away to do so, and he never takes enough for his victims to notice, curing their bite marks with his blood and compelling away their memories of having met him. It doesn't upset me that he does it, though I know he avoids talking about it with me, but he's never hidden it either. I know what Antoine is, and he knows that I know. "Hunting animals," says Jeremiah.

"Animals?" Now I'm really confused.

"Yes, Harper." Jeremiah sounds slightly impatient. "Animals. The great American pastimes: hunting, fishing, and trapping."

"Oh." I feel mildly foolish. "I guess I just didn't know he did that."

Jeremiah gives me an odd look. "It doesn't bother you that he hunts people—but animals bother you?"

I shrug, feeling stupid. I can't explain it, exactly, except to say that hunting, when Antoine has no actual need or desire to eat what he catches, seems to me both unnecessary and out of character. I feel a faint chill under my skin. It seems another indication of Keziah's influence.

On cue, I hear the sound of Antoine's truck in the driveway, and a moment later he is standing in the kitchen.

"Was that your new family member I passed, jogging down the road toward town?" he says by way of greeting.

"Callie," I nod. "And she may need your help at some point. I suspect we may get a visit from Social Services that will require some—persuasion."

"You want me to compel government officials?" He raises his eyebrows at me. "Are you sure your brother will be okay with that?"

"Connor and I aren't in a great place." I fill him and Jeremiah in on last night's exchange.

"Connor will come round," says Jeremiah confidently, picking up his helmet and getting ready to leave. "He's just having a hard time, is all."

"I'm getting a little tired of hearing about what a hard time Connor is having," I say testily. "He's not the only one facing challenges." Too late, I realize how that comment might be interpreted. Clearly Jeremiah does too. He makes a hasty exit, leaving me alone with Antoine, who is regarding me with a carefully neutral expression.

"I wasn't implying that we're facing challenges." I feel my face redden.

"*Challenges* seems a remarkably inadequate term for what we face." I'm relieved when he smiles. "And while we're discussing challenges, care to tell me who it is I'm supposed to be compelling? What story are we telling people about Callie? More importantly, what story are we *telling* Callie?" This time his smile is a little strained.

"I know it's awkward," I say apologetically.

He makes a rather choked sound. "Awkward is one way of putting it. How long do you think we'll manage to hide the awkward fact that I, Tate, and your brother's girlfriend are vampires? Or how about the awkward facts that a pack of wolves live over the river, and an ancient creature of indeterminate origin would like us all dead?"

"You forgot the awkward facts about me," I say. "The weird unknown nature spirit Keziah wants to take alive, by all accounts."

"And then there is that."

"I'm glad we can laugh about it."

"Who's laughing?" Pushing away from the doorframe, Antoine moves restlessly around the kitchen. "But I guess you're right. We can't put her out on the street, or not yet, at least." Is it my imagination, I wonder, or is he more unsettled than normal? "I need to meet with Tate today." He looks past me, out the window. "But I'll be back in time for dinner. I can pick something up in town if you like. For Callie, too."

I nod slowly. "I thought Tate had already left," I say to the wall of his back. He swings around, as if startled, then just as quickly turns away again. When he speaks there's an odd note to his voice, and I know, with a horrible dread, that he's lying when he says: "Not yet, no. He flies out tonight."

Since I already know that Tate flew out last night, there isn't much I can say to that, and so I stay quiet until Antoine leaves shortly afterward.

A storm is gathering on the horizon, but it's no more than puffy clouds for now, and I spend the day in the water garden, pushing bulbs into the silt. Nothing has emerged above the surface yet. These bulbs are for water lilies, soft-colored flowers I've always loved. If the lotus bulbs hold the promise of rich, sensual flowers, lilies always remind me of innocence and joy. "They're like the babies of the flower world," I tell Callie when she returns from Deepwater later that day and comes to sit on the riverbank. "Sweet smelling, clean, and new to the world."

"Are y'all having a kid? You and whatever-his-name-is, your husband?"

I'm so startled by the question I almost fall over in the river. I'm very glad I have my back to Callie. I'm afraid those piercing blue eyes would see straight through me when I say carefully, "We haven't really talked about it."

"Well, that's kinda weird, ain't it? Who in the world gets

married at your age unless there's a baby involved, somewhere in the piece?"

"Us, I guess." Composing my face, I turn, give her a bright smile, and change the subject. "How did your job interview go?"

"It wasn't an interview, as such. I just waited for the boss to show up and offered to work for nothing for a day." She shrugs. "I got a job at the end of it. I usually do."

"Usually?" I smile at her. "You sound like you've had a lot of jobs."

"Sure." She plucks grass from the bank and tears it apart between fingers with short, clipped nails. "Been workin' since I could walk, more or less. Always work if you want it. My best job was at Beale Boxing, though." A wistful look passes over her face. "I liked it there," she says quietly. "Gonna miss that place, for sure."

"A boxing studio?" I ask curiously.

She nods. "Been training there since I was eight. Started off cleaning their floors."

"Eight?" I stare at her. She stares back.

"I tol' you," she says flatly. "My momma was no good. And 'sides, that part of Memphis, you learn to fight early, and you learn to fight good. Otherwise you end up dead real early on, you feel me?"

"I guess so." But the reality is, I don't. For all that Tessa, Connor, and I never had much, we'd always had enough, and Mom had always had a job. I can't imagine what it would have been like to grow up without knowing that kind of security. I feel vaguely ashamed that I didn't somehow know about Callie earlier, that all that time I was living with her brother in a nice apartment in Baton Rouge, Callie had been learning to fight in a hard suburb of Memphis.

"It's not your fault." She's watching me with uncanny perception. "Just the way life is, you know? And I ain't your responsibility now, neither." She stands up and brushes the grass from her legs.

"Noted." I smile as I wade out of the water. "But if you're hungry, Antoine is bringing dinner from Deepwater tonight. I can hear his truck now. You're welcome to share it."

"Sure." She says it lightly, but I suppress another smile as I see how eagerly she walks toward the mansion. Something tells me that for all her bravado, regular meals aren't something Callie Lafayette is used to.

CHAPTER 5

KILLER

ntoine has brought Jeremiah with him, and we eat in a companionable group on the back porch, overlooking the river. "You don't mind if I stay here tonight, do you, Harper?" Jeremiah doesn't even look up when I say it's fine. He's been spending more time here ever since Connor's departure, and I like having him around. He and Callie are immersed in a conversation about a social media app I've never even heard of. I've never really bothered with social media. It's always seemed like something that belongs to a world I'm not part of, even more so since we came to Deepwater. I can't imagine what kind of things I'd post there, anyway. Jeremiah and Callie, however, seem completely absorbed and are soon cackling with delight over some video involving someone dressed up like a rabbit impersonating various films.

The fact that I don't understand the appeal makes me feel as if I'm a thousand years old, not eighteen.

"We didn't celebrate your birthday," says Antoine, when I mention this to him as we take the dishes inside.

I shrug. "I wasn't really in the mood." It had been back in March. I'm still not ready to celebrate the day Tessa and I were born. Sometimes I wonder if I ever will be again. Talk of birthdays and age just makes me realise how much has happened since the last time I stood around blowing candles out. I feel as if I should have been done with school a long time ago. I am more than eager for senior year to be over.

"We should celebrate, one night. Go somewhere special."

"You know," I say, as he wraps his arms around me, "I still don't feel much in the mood for parties, after the last two events we've attended."

Antoine smiles ruefully. "I guess I can understand that."

"Antoine." I meet his eyes. "Where were you today?"

I feel him tense, see the opaque mask I've come to dread fall over his eyes. He steps back from me. "I told you. I met with Tate."

"Tate flew out of Jackson last night." I know I should let it go, but I can't. "Jeremiah said you've been . . . hunting. A lot. Is that where you were? Hunting?"

"Does it matter if I was?"

"It does if you need to lie about it." We're standing with a foot between us now, and my heart is beating uncomfortably fast. I don't like the detached expression on his face, the hard light in his eyes.

"Maybe there are some things about what I am that you don't need to understand." He looks at me with something almost like contempt. "Some things you *can't* understand, Harper." His words hurt almost as much as Connor's did yesterday, and I'm about to push past him and ask him to leave when he catches my arm. When I swing around to face him, his face is so agonized my anger melts away.

"I'm sorry," he says roughly. "I don't know why I said that. I don't even know who I am half the time—" his voice breaks off, and he rubs a hand over his face.

"It's Keziah." I move closer to him, putting my hand on his

face. "It's her doing this to you. Please, Antoine—won't you at least think about taking some of my blood?"

"No." He shakes his head once, but with the stern finality that is all too familiar. "Don't ask that, Harper. I can't."

I step closer to him and wordlessly twine my arms around his neck.

For a moment he is still and taut, holding himself apart from me, then as I press against him he groans, his arms pulling me into him as he takes my mouth fiercely, and I know that if nothing else, at least I can give him this comfort, the refuge of my body.

LATE THAT NIGHT, I WAKE TO FIND HIM GONE, THE BED EMPTY and windows wide open, the wind billowing the curtains. A storm is gathering. I pick up my wrap and pad downstairs, thinking I will find him where I often do, standing on the back porch looking down at the river.

But he isn't there, though his truck is still out front.

I search the mansion room by room, growing increasingly confused, until finally there is only the library left. I pause. It's been weeks since I've gone into that room; it holds too many memories, none of them good. Finally I push open the door.

Antoine is here, I know it. I can feel him on the air. And even if I couldn't, the bookshelf yawns open, exposing the dark staircase behind it leading down to the cellar.

I pull the wrap about me tightly. Why would Antoine be in the cellar? "Antoine," I call softly, moving closer to the staircase. "Antoine, are you down there?"

He doesn't answer, but I can sense him, and when I peer down into the gloom, I think I can hear him moving around. "Antoine?"

"Harper." There is something so weary and resigned in his voice, I don't think twice before racing down the stairs toward him. He's clad in nothing more than jeans, his torso bare, standing in the cellar with his back to me and his head down, his posture so uncharacteristically defeated a bolt of dread goes through me. "What is it?" I come up behind him. "What's wrong?"

He spins around, so fast I don't even have time to step back, and I know immediately I should never have come down the stairs, that this isn't the man I married, nor any other version of Antoine I know.

This is the face of a killer—and he's coming for me.

I scream, but I already know it's too late, because he planned this, and I'm no match for the vampire he is.

This time, when his arms come around me, there's nothing gentle about his embrace. It's hard and unyielding. Deathly. Then, just as I think he will crush me with iron strength, he steps back, his expression shifting, changing, going from blank hardness to horrified awareness. He staggers back, staring at me, and puts out a hand as if to ward me off.

"Harper," he says thickly. "I have to leave. Now. I have to go." Before I can so much as protest, he is backing up the stairs, still watching me. "You're not hurt," he says, his voice rasping. "Tell me you're not hurt."

"No!" I move toward him, but he waves me away so fiercely I stop. "I'm not hurt, Antoine," I protest. "You didn't hurt me."

"I'm leaving. You won't see me for a time, Harper. Not until I've worked out how to get this under control. You're not safe, do you understand?" He glances around wildly, as if he can hear something I can't. "In the box on the porch," he says hoarsely, "there is frankincense. Burn it in every room of the house. Jeremiah will show you how. Put it in your water. Whatever you do, Harper, keep the mansion—and yourself—protected, do you understand?" I'm following him up the stairs, but as fast as I come, he moves faster, never letting me get close enough to touch him.

"Please don't go," I plead. "My blood will fix this, Antoine, you know it will. Just take a little. Enough to help you see clearly."

"I can't." He says it with such finality I stop, looking at him. "Keziah wants me to drain you, Harper." His voice is weary, coming from deep within him. "She wants to turn you, and she wants me to be the one who kills you. If I start drinking from you, I won't be strong enough to stop." He shakes his head as I come closer. "I have to go," he says hoarsely, his eyes red rimmed and exhausted. "Do you understand, Harper? I have to leave, and I can't come back. And no matter what I say to you, no matter how I beg, Harper, you have to promise you won't come after me."

When I pause, he stands at the kitchen door, and I can almost feel the tension within him, the impossible battle as he tries to fight Keziah's pull. "Promise me," he says roughly. "Whatever you do, Harper, don't come after me."

We stare at each other for a long moment. Then he arches, his body bent in a spasm so savage and painful it hurts me to look at it, and I cry out, my hands reaching for him but finding only air.

"Promise!" He almost shouts the word, and I realize he is hanging on until it is almost killing him, and tears are running down my cheeks, and I don't know what else to do, and as the wind outside picks up and lightning shoots from the sky, he gasps with pain, and I say it.

"I promise!" I scream brokenly into the wind. I slump down on the uneven porch boards as the summer storm breaks overhead. "I promise I won't come after you, Antoine."

And then he is gone.

My tears mingle with the musty river water raining down upon me, until Callie and Jeremiah come and make me come inside.

CHAPTER 6

HONESTY

I wake to a dawn washed clean by the storm, the slope leading to the jetty strewn with fallen magnolia petals. I don't remember how I got to bed. I have vague recollections of Jeremiah's stricken face and whispered questions, my own inability to so much as form a word other than *no* when he asked if I was hurt. Callie I recall only as a blur in the background, silent and unobtrusive, and when I wake it is to find her on the jetty again, performing her exercises as if nothing more has happened than a little overnight rain.

I shower, dress, and walk down to the jetty, carrying two mugs of coffee. She is just finishing her punishing routine of push-ups and planks. She takes the coffee without comment, and we sit in the growing dawn, watching the river.

"I'm sorry about last night," I say at last.

"No need."

Her reply is so nonchalant I glance sideways. Her pointed face is closed and unreadable, the blue eyes as blank as a summer sky. "I wish I could explain," I begin. "It's complicated, I guess."

Callie makes a dismissive sound that stops me. "No need." She sips her coffee and looks straight ahead. "I've seen worse." She shrugs. "At least he's beating on you, not me. You want my advice, though, I'd change the locks. Ain't nobody need that in their life." I'm so taken aback I don't know whether to laugh or cry.

"You don't understand," I say, trying to keep my voice steady. "Antoine wasn't—hurting me. He'd never do that."

"Sure." She sips her coffee and shrugs again. "Whatever. Like I said: ain't none of my business."

I open my mouth to protest then close it again. Much as it pains me to cast Antoine in the role of domestic abuser, it's as good a cover as any, I guess, and at least it saves me from inventing yet more lies. I sip more coffee. After a short silence, I say: "You train hard. Where did you learn to do all that?"

"Beale Boxing," she says briefly.

"The place you worked? Was it on Beale Street, then?" I've heard of the famous music strip in Memphis, like everyone else. Callie laughs, perhaps the first genuine humor I've heard from her since she arrived.

"Hell, no." She's still chuckling. "Ain't no place for someone like me, place like that. Beale Street's for fancy white tourists." I'm tempted to point out that Callie is, in fact, white, but by the way her accent thickens every time she talks about Memphis, I'm guessing her skin color was something she worked hard to disguise in her old life. "Beale Boxing is out in Shelby Forest-Frayser." At my blank expression her smile fades. "Let's just say the only thing it has in common with downtown is the crime rate. Only in Shelby, it ain't wallets people is after—and their guns ain't for show." She pokes moodily at the dirt with one foot.

"So you trained in this boxing studio, then?" It's easier talking about Callie's life than my own.

"Sure did. Lanie trained me from age eight. For free, too."

"Was that where you got that sword you train with?"

Callie gives me a sharp look. When I don't look away, she nods briefly. "It was a present. On my tenth birthday, after I won a tournament. Used to be Lanie's."

"Was Lanie a good man?"

"Weren't no man." Callie gives me a wry smile. "Lanie was the toughest lady in Shelby."

"Was?" I regret the question as soon as I see her face cloud over.

"Drive by," Callie says shortly. "Meant to hit one of the boys who trained there. Hit Lanie instead." There doesn't seem much to say to that, so silence falls between us again that is broken a short time later by the sound of a car in the drive.

I try not to run up the slope, even though I know before I reach the house that the engine isn't that of Antoine's truck. Jeremiah comes downstairs yawning and scratching his head at the same time I burst onto the porch to find Avery stepping out of her hatchback, looking as impeccably groomed as ever. Sunglasses are pushed back on her head and long brown legs gleam under a light cotton dress so short that Jeremiah goes crimson and backs away into the house, muttering an awkward greeting as he retreats upstairs, to Callie's visible amusement.

Avery isn't smiling. Her eyes cut to Callie then back to me. "Can we talk?" she says without preamble.

I turn to make excuses, but Callie, as shrewd as ever, has already disappeared. I lead Avery upstairs to my room, and she perches on one of the window seats, her beauty making the entire room look like something from a decor magazine. "You need to speak to Antoine."

I'm still trying to think of a response when she carries on in a flurry of words. "Or at least to Connor. Things can't go on like this."

"Like what?" I ask cautiously.

"Cass," says Avery bluntly, as if the name in itself should be self-explanatory. "She's getting worse. Bodies are mounting up, Harper. The wolves can't keep covering for her, no matter what Connor orders them to do. I thought that now, with Antoine going there and all, you must be on better terms. Maybe Antoine can talk to her."

"Antoine's there? At Connor's?" In an instant I'm at her side. "Is he there now?"

Avery's face darkens. "Seriously, Harper?" She shakes her head. "I tell you that our ex-best friend is murdering bayou people, that your brother is forcing the wolves to cover for her, and that's your question?"

"I'm sorry." I slump down on my bed. "Really, Avery. I am. That was thoughtless." When her stony expression doesn't change, I go on clumsily, "Antoine and I had a—fight, last night. About Keziah. He ran into the night, and I haven't seen him since."

"A fight," says Avery flatly.

"A little more than a fight, actually." I meet her eyes. "Keziah is summoning him again. It's been happening for a while, getting harder for him to resist. He's changing, Avery. Becoming someone I don't even know. Maybe the same thing is happening to Cass."

Avery's face is still hard. "Be that as it may, if Cass keeps killing people, it doesn't matter who is ordering her to do it. The wolves will need to take her down."

"Take her down?" I feel my heart skip a beat.

"Vampires are the traditional enemies of wolves," Avery says. When I glance around warily and put a finger on my lips, she makes an impatient noise. "I'm done keeping your secrets, Harper. And you should be, too. Anyone near you is in danger. The least you can do is be honest." Since I don't know how to argue with that, I stay quiet. Avery barely glances up when Jeremiah sidles into my room and stands by the door, listening. "Like I said," Avery goes on in the same loud voice, "the wolf spirit is designed to keep the tribe safe from predators. *Any* predators. Including vampires. It's unnatural for them to be near vampires, to tolerate them in their midst. And now not only is one of those vampires killing our own, but the wolf leading the pack is not one of our people—and is more focused on protecting his vampire girlfriend than the people she's killing."

Despite my concern for Connor, I can see how this would cause problems, and my understanding must show on my face because Avery nods, and for the first time I can see the desperation behind her eyes. "Remy is the pack's natural leader," she says, in a slightly less hostile tone. "He knows the wolves. They're his people, his brothers, his blood. Connor isn't one of them. He just . . . rules them. Like a—" she waves her hand in the air, searching for the word.

"Dictator?" Jeremiah offers.

"Exactly." Avery doesn't so much as glance at him. "Like a dictator. He orders them to follow Cass, to protect her, when their every instinct is to kill her. He doesn't spend time with the wolves, doesn't care about their problems or their families, how hard it is for them to come to terms with what they are, to keep their secret. It's Remy who picks up those pieces, who stops them falling into alcohol and drugs and confusion, who has to find money for their families and cover for them when they miss work." She looks at me. "Antoine used to be able to get Cass under control. I thought that's why he went there last night, to talk to her."

I shake my head. "I wish that were true. But I suspect he's gone there because he's hearing Keziah again and wants to know if Cass is, too." I frown. "Are you certain it's Cass who is killing people? Not Keziah?"

"Both, I'm guessing, though Keziah we haven't seen. Whereas

Cass—" Avery breaks off and for the first time I see real despair on her face. "Cass isn't even careful, Harper," she says. "She simply doesn't seem to care. And Connor just runs alongside her, as if the people she hunts are no more than food to collect in the supermarket."

The image is so chilling I feel my stomach twist.

"You have to talk to your brother, Harper. Or do something yourself." The anger is gone from Avery's face and she just sounds tired. "I've done everything I know how to do. The protection spells Lori has shown me, everything Noya whispers from the spirit world. But to be honest, I just don't really have that kind of power. I don't have the ability to protect people like you do." A touch of resentment is in her voice as she looks at me. "Is there something you can do?"

"Maybe if I was fully in control of whatever it is that I am." I feel the familiar impotence wash over me. "But I'm not. I don't even understand how it works, not really."

"But surely Antoine must know?"

I shake my head, reluctant to tell her what Antoine has told me, remembering his warnings. Some of my thoughts must show on my face, because Avery's closes over, and she stands up abruptly. "I came here to ask for help," she says. "But it seems clear I won't get any, so you better hear what I'm saying, Harper. Sooner rather than later, the wolves are going to rebel. If they have to go through Connor to stop Cass, the wolves will do it. Unless you want to lose your brother as well as our friend—and possibly your husband, as well—you're going to have to find a way to turn this around. Because it can't go on, do you understand? Vampires can't just kill people in the bayous and get away with it. It isn't right, and we won't stand by anymore and watch it happen."

Without waiting for a reply, she swings off the window seat and pushes past Jeremiah. We stare at each other as we hear her stalk downstairs, the sound of her car starting up. In the silence following her departure, the sound of a door swinging open makes us both spin around. It's the bathroom adjoining my room. Callie is standing there, looking between us with sharp, serious blue eyes.

"I think y'all better tell me what's going on," she says.

CHAPTER 7

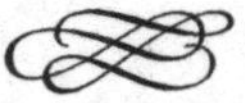

TRAINING

"So let me get this straight." It's evening, and Jeremiah, Callie, and I are sitting on the back porch, looking down to where the river is turned to moving flame by the orange dusk. "Your husband and the history teacher at school are both vampires—but good ones." Callie's voice is oddly matter-of-fact. "This Keziah is also a vampire, but one that can't be killed. Or at least, you don't know how to kill her yet. She used to be trapped in your cellar by a curse, which is why you"—she nods at me—"had to marry Antoine, who is also a vampire. To keep the curse intact. Then Keziah escaped, but you stayed married to this vampire anyhow. Your brother Connor turns into a wolf, same as Avery's boyfriend, but not the same as them, because he was made, not born. *His* girlfriend, this Cass, is also a vampire. She likes killing people, but we still think she's one of the good ones. Am I right, so far?" She stares at me and I nod, somewhat awkwardly. It's hard hearing it all put down so brutally.

"And you," she says, still looking at me, "you're some kind of . . . what did you call it?"

"Nature spirit," says Jeremiah helpfully.

"Right." Callie sips a soda meditatively and looks at the river. "You know, when you told me this morning that y'all would explain it to me after work, I spent the day kind of thinking I must have misunderstood what I heard. I'm not sure what's weirder. The fact that I actually convinced myself I'd misheard, or the fact that everything I heard was right."

Her accent, I notice absently, has disappeared almost entirely, just as her entire grammatical construction has altered. Callie's mannerisms, it seems, are just another part of her mask.

"So what happens now?"

I look at her, confused. "What do you mean?"

"Well, what are we going to do?" Callie looks between Jeremiah and me. "Y'all have some kind of plan, don't you?"

"Callie," I start, exchanging an awkward glance with Jeremiah, "I thought that after we explained all of this that you'd want to leave."

"It isn't safe here," Jeremiah adds. He nods at the frankincense resin smoking atop coals in dishes set about the porch. There's a small lump inside our soda cans, lending a eucalyptus-type flavor to the liquid, and we've all rubbed the oil behind our ears and on our wrists. "This isn't just for show. Sooner or later, vampires will come here. It's more than possible they will be under Keziah's control. You could die, Callie. We all could."

"Sure." The accent is back, and Callie swigs her can with a hint of her customary bravado. "Coulda died any day in Shelby Forest. Plenty did. Good people. Friends." She drinks again, but this time the swagger is missing. "Least here, it's supernatural things tryin' to kill us. Not Momma's latest boyfriend, or drugged-out freaks just shootin' for fun." There's a shadow in the deep blue eyes, and it brings home to me that Callie, in her short life, has seen more death and violence than even Jeremiah or me. "Seems to me," she goes on, "the real problem y'all have is this Keziah creature. If it's her controlling yo' man," she nods at me, "and y'all's friend, then seems simple enough. We need to find a way to take her down. Stop her running the play, y'all feelin' me?"

I suppress a smile. "I'm feeling you," I say. "But Keziah is old. Older than anyone else. And nobody knows how to kill her."

"But your man Tate, he's gone to Haiti to find out, true?"

"He's following a lead." Jeremiah shrugs. "No guarantee he'll find answers."

"People," says Callie in an exasperated tone, glancing between us. "A little optimism, please."

"Fine." I'm smiling, despite myself and all the awful things that have happened in the past day or so. "What do you suggest, then, Callie?"

"Way I see it, we got a few things we can do." She holds up a hand and starts ticking fingers off. "We can try to find out why this Keziah wants you so bad, Harper. What exactly you are. That's work for Jeremiah and me." Jeremiah looks up, surprise flaring briefly in his eyes, but he sits a little straighter and doesn't argue. "It's clear I'm gonna need to train y'all," Callie goes on, ticking off another finger. "I'm not staying in a house with two people who can't so much as throw a punch." This makes me particularly happy.

"You'll train us?" I try not to sound too eager. "I wanted to ask if you would." I meet Jeremiah's eyes. "I'm so sick of feeling helpless."

He nods. "You're not the only one."

"Well, I'll train y'all. But I promise you—" Callie fixes us with a stern eye "—it ain't gonna be easy." She looks away. "There's one more thing." Her voice has lost the authority of a moment before. "Your brother."

"Our brother," I correct her.

She shrugs. "Maybe. Maybe not." When she looks at me, I see the defensiveness in her eyes, and I realize this, at least, isn't a front. Connor isn't anything to Callie. Not yet. All he is, so far, is just another person who has let her down. The thought breaks my heart more than I imagined it could.

"You're gonna need to talk to him," she goes on. "Try changing his mind."

"I can try. But he loves Cass. More than anything—or anyone—else."

Callie doesn't answer that. Nobody does. There isn't, at the moment, an argument to make.

AFTER THAT CONVERSATION, TIME SLIPS AWAY HORRIBLY QUICKLY. I'm both grateful and concerned at how fast the end of the school year approaches. Between Callie's ruthless training timetable and final exams, I'm so busy I barely even attend to the water garden. When I do manage to visit it, all I see is still water, no sign of lily or lotus. Maybe, I think, the bulbs haven't taken. I'm not sure whether to feel sad or happy about that. Maybe I don't have any special power, after all. Maybe it's all just a myth.

But in the final week, with only my history exam left, time seems to slow once more, and I sit in the late afternoon sun after school, working my hands into the earth. At first I simply enjoy the feel of the dirt under my fingers, the warmth of the sun on my back. Then, as the day fades, I seem to slip into a different space, the place between time I only ever find in painting or gardening, and I barely notice it when night falls.

"Wow." When Callie's voice pulls me out of my trance, night is deep, the moon high over the river. She isn't looking at me, but at the plants around me, her eyes wide and fascinated. I follow her gaze, but I can't really see anything unusual, just plants I've tended.

"What?" I say.

She pulls her eyes back to me and looks at me curiously. "You don't see it?"

"See what?"

"Jeremiah," Callie says, pulling him forward. The two of them seem to go everywhere together these days, like a matched pair. "Tell her."

"I told you," Jeremiah says. "She never seems to notice."

"Notice what?" I'm growing impatient.

"This morning when we left for school," Callie says, staring at me with an odd expression, "there were no flowers at all in this part of the garden. And now—" she gestures at the circle where I've been working. I follow her finger. From the newly turned earth rise a variety of spring flowers: periwinkle, iris, pinkroot, all wide open, in full bloom.

"They were here already," I say defensively. "I just helped them along a little."

"No, Harper," says Jeremiah quietly. "None of them were here. I don't think I've ever even seen any of them grow here before."

I open my mouth to protest, but Callie puts a hand on my arm. "It ain't a bad thing," she says, in as soft a voice as I've ever heard her use. "You got powers, Harper. Maybe instead of fighting them, you should try using them." I look between her and Jeremiah.

"I have no idea how to use them. It drives me crazy." It does. To know that I have something that everyone seems to want, something strong enough to fight off Caleb, yet not truly know how to use it, makes me feel frustrated and helpless.

"Well, there's nothing stopping you trying, at least." Callie gestures around at the garden. "Maybe just try doing this again. But next time, see if you can think on it a little. Imagine it like that dang frankincense y'all burn everywhere." Her mouth twists in distaste. Callie isn't a fan of the frankincense we make her put in the water. "It's like fighting," she explains.

"You gotta imagine your strike falling the right way, play it out in your head. Who knows? Maybe it might work for your powers, too."

For the next few days, I do as she suggests, and though I can't be certain, it seems to me that in the places where I work that way, the grass is darker, the flowers stronger. I work at the edges of the mansion, imagining my hands digging a border of protection around our land, envisaging it keeping us safe. Somewhere inside me I feel a deep fear that my border is also keeping Antoine out; but I push that thought from my mind and dig away, using the work to block out the pain and loneliness of his absence.

Whatever power I may or may not have doesn't mean a thing when it comes to Callie's training.

"Come on," she yells at me in the early morning before my final exam. We're running along the road into Deepwater, and the breath is rasping so hard in my throat it feels like razor blades. Beside me, Jeremiah is faring no better. "You can't fight if you ain't fit! And you two are about as fit as burned hamburger on a plate! Move!"

I'm not sure what is more annoying—having orders barked at me by a skinny girl child, or the colorful metaphors said child comes up with to describe our lack of fitness. "If you're so fit," I pant at her, "maybe you could expend some energy doing housework once in a while." She doesn't deign to answer this, continuing to harangue Jeremiah and I all the way into Deepwater.

I reach school sweating so horribly that Mr. Larkin, who is overseeing my history exam, looks at me in distaste. "I will say, Miss Ellory," he says in a dry tone, "that while I might be glad you seem to have reconsidered the company you keep, your personal hygiene has taken a distinct downturn."

"What *has* happened to your boyfriend, Harper?" It's Jared, his eyes gleaming as he takes in my sweaty T-shirt clinging to my body. I almost roll my eyes. Only Jared Baudelaire could hit on a girl dripping in sweat.

"He's just gone away for a time, is all." I turn away, using a towel to dry my face and neck.

"Sure." Jared sounds unconvinced. "Like Cass Charles has gone away, and your brother. Connor, isn't it?" I don't have an answer to that. Connor hasn't been by the mansion in weeks, since Callie arrived, in fact. I know she takes his absence personally, even if she doesn't speak of it. I'm not sure what hurts me more: Connor's absence or Antoine's. I've tried calling Tate, but to no avail. Seems like cell reception in Haiti isn't quite what he promised it would be. He must be getting emails though, since my classmates all seem to have received responses to their queries.

All except me. Tate hasn't answered so much as one of my emails.

"Seems like lots of people are disappearing lately." I realize Jared is watching me as he says this. "And like other people are just showing up." His eyes settle on Callie, passing by in the opposite breezeway on her way to class. "Who is the gutter trash, anyhow? Talks like something out of a ghetto."

"Callie is family."

"Oh, yeah?" Jared sneers. "Whose family?"

"Mine." I glare at him fiercely. "And if I hear that any of you are being any less than kind to her, I'll tell your mother, Jared, that it was you who supplied all the weed at the party that got broken up two weeks ago, and then went and blamed it on boys from the bayou. Who got charged with possession, I might add. Falsely." I stare at him until he colors and backs off, muttering, but neutralized, at least for now. I don't want anyone asking awkward questions about Callie, particularly now that I no longer have a vampire available to compel the questions away.

I look up to find Callie staring at me. Two high spots of color show on her cheeks, and her blue eyes seem for a moment to glisten in the sunlight. Then she turns and is gone, without so much as a nod in my direction.

That afternoon, however, I return to the mansion to find burgers grilling on the porch and every surface in the mansion swept and mopped.

CHAPTER 8

FIGHTING

The morning after my final exam, Antoine comes to the mansion.

I don't initially realize he is there. Callie is training Jeremiah and me down on the jetty. We're sparring, practicing the strike and defend moves she's taught us, and I'm so absorbed in avoiding Jeremiah's increasingly accurate movements that I don't hear the truck pull up. It's only when I spin and come up to find Antoine glowering at me from the end of the jetty that I freeze, meaning Jeremiah's last blow lands squarely on my shoulder.

"Ow," I say, rubbing it.

"Why didn't you move? You were supposed to move." He catches sight of Antoine. "Oh." Jeremiah raises one hand awkwardly in a greeting that Antoine doesn't return. Callie turns to see what he's waving at.

"Hey," she says, without much enthusiasm. "You're back."

Antoine ignores them both. His eyes are trained on me. "What do you think you're doing?" he asks in a cold voice.

"Callie is training us to fight." I let my eyes drop to the frankincense burning in pots at the end of the jetty, right in front of him. "We're learning how to protect ourselves," I say pointedly. "Just like you told me."

"Frankincense is protection. Fighting is ridiculous." He glares at Jeremiah. "I would have thought you, at least, would have more brains."

"That's an odd assumption," says Jeremiah just as coldly, folding his arms in a gesture startlingly reminiscent of Antoine's own. "Since you haven't bothered to so much as call to find out how I did on my final exams."

"Forgive me if I've had other things on my mind." There's no softening in Antoine's expression, nothing at all of his usual wry humor, the twisted smile I love so much. This man is the stranger I've seen before, the hard, cold creature that belongs not to magnolias and sunlight, but to Keziah and death.

"Why are you here?" I ask quietly. 'What do you want, Antoine?"

"Have you spoken to Tate?" He answers my question with one of his own.

I shake my head. "He isn't answering my calls or emails."

Antoine's mouth tightens. "Nor mine."

"Why?" I counter, holding his eyes. "What do you need from Tate?"

"I need him to take you away from here." His eyes roam over us. "All of you."

Jeremiah steps forward. "Well, we've no intention of going." He stares down Antoine defiantly. "And unless you've learned how to outsmart frankincense, you can't compel any of us to leave or physically cross the end of this jetty. We've all been practically mainlining the stuff. It's burning in every corner of the property."

Antoine glares at him. "Frankincense won't keep Keziah out for long."

"It's kept her out so far," Jeremiah says stubbornly. "And besides—Harper has been practicing using her powers on the ground here. There's more protecting this land than just frank-incense now." I wince as I see Antoine's eyes narrow. They swivel to me.

"Is that true?" His voice is dangerously quiet.

"Why?" It's Callie's turn to speak now. "Are you going to beat on her if she says yes?"

Antoine's expression is so taken aback that it's almost comi-cal. For a moment he actually seems to lose his power of speech. I take advantage of his shock by interrupting. "I'm not sure if it's working or not," I say. "I've been trying to focus on the ground here, working with the earth, the trees and plants on our border. I don't really know what I'm doing, obviously. But it seems to be working." I gesture around at the ground and Antoine follows my arm, his eyes narrowing again as he takes in the lush grasses, the blooms rising from every available source. Only the water garden remains stubbornly closed to me, although green shoots are showing just under the surface. I'd already planted the bulbs when I read that they should have been put in more shallow water. I've resigned myself to losing them.

"We're not certain what she should do," adds Jeremiah. "But we're fairly sure we'd be a lot safer if you'd give her your blood —activate her, like you did the wolves." Antoine's eyes flare and he clenches his fists.

"There he goes again," says Callie, shaking her head. "Don't clench your fists at me, mister. I've taken on worse than you and come off better."

I bite my lip to stifle a grin, but the impulse dies as soon as I look at Antoine's face. Normally, I know, he'd be unable to resist grinning back at me. But there's no trace of humor on his face. Nothing but detachment and cold, hard anger.

"You told them about my blood activating you?" He throws the words at me like stones.

"Yes, I told them." I don't flinch. "They're my friends,

Antoine. My family. The people who are standing with me, regardless of what it might cost them."

"Then they can hear this as well." His eyes shift to each of them fleetingly before coming back to rest on me. "Playing with power you don't understand isn't just dangerous. It's insane. It can attract things you don't expect, draw the attention of creatures none of us have ever even heard of yet. It isn't something to play with, to make experiments of. It's something you should forget about and keep hidden, if you want to stay alive." Every one of his words cuts me inside, as if by rejecting what power I have, he is also rejecting a part of my own soul. "You need to get out of here," he says, his eyes moving between us. "All of you. That's what I came to say. I've bought a van big enough for you to take what you will need." *That's why I didn't hear his truck*, I think vaguely, then wonder why I think it matters what I did or didn't hear, when my husband is effectively ordering me out of his life. "Don't tell anyone where you are going, not even Connor or Avery. The fewer people who know you've left, the safer you'll be."

"But you'll know," I say quietly. "And since it's clear that you're under Keziah's control, it seems particularly stupid to do anything you tell us to. How do we know you aren't already acting on her orders?" His face is flat and hard, his expression unchanging as I take a step toward him.

"Harper," says Jeremiah warningly as I near the frankincense barrier at the end of the jetty.

"It's okay, Jeremiah." I'm still holding Antoine's eyes. "If you let me have some of your blood," I say softly, "I can protect not just the mansion, but all of us. I can feel it, Antoine. In my body. As if something inside me is just waiting to wake up. Something so strong and powerful—" I cut myself off, but not before I see an odd light wake in his eyes. I feel a surge of hope. "I don't know that I even realized it before I started trying to use it." It's true. Until the last few weeks, the power they all spoke about had felt oddly separate to me, a kind of theoretical thing that might or might not have been real. But in the days since I've begun visualizing it, as Callie suggested, I can sense it moving through me, a flow both fascinating and terrifying, something that is part of me and also separate, like an untapped spring lying beneath the earth. "I'm strong, Antoine. Stronger than any of you understand. All I need is your blood, and all of this can be over. I know it."

"Harper." He shakes his head wearily, and for a fleeting moment I see a hint of the man I know beneath the hard facade. "None of us know *what* you will be if you take my blood. We can't know. It's more than possible that giving you my blood is exactly what Keziah wants." He flinches, and I feel it, the horrible pull of her mind on his. When he looks up, his eyes are burning coals again, and I take an involuntary step backwards. His lips harden into a thin line. "I'm barely holding on, Harper." His words are forced through gritted teeth. "I hardly even know who I am most of the time. I can't come here again. I don't know—" he bites off the words, but I know what he's trying to say.

"You don't know if it's you who decided to come here, or if you're here because she sent you."

He nods curtly. "You have to leave, Harper." His voice cracks on my name. "You have to leave, and you have to go somewhere I can't find you. Where no one can find you." He looks bleakly around at us all. "Take care of her. Take care of each other. But go. Please, go."

Then he strides off up the slope, and we stand in the growing day, staring through the haze of frankincense until his tall, hard figure is gone from sight.

CHAPTER 9

FAMILY

"What do you think we should do?"

The three of us are sitting in the kitchen, where we've been since Antoine left that morning. It's afternoon now, and we've been going around in the same circles since the moment we sat down. The table is littered with the empty soda cans and snack packets Callie and Jeremiah seem to have an insatiable appetite for and pieces of paper on which we've written pros and cons. I've found it hard to eat anything. I can't stop thinking about the shifting shadows in Antoine's eyes, the way the man I know he is keeps breaking through the hold Keziah has on him, then disappearing again. I want to reach inside his body and pull Keziah out of him, stamp her into the earth until she is no more than ash. Keziah feels like a cancer eating the man I love from the inside out. It's killing me to watch.

"I can't leave," I say, for what must be the tenth time. "Everything that matters in my life is here. I'm not going anywhere."

"But what if Antoine's right?" Jeremiah argues, as he, also, has since this morning. "What if by being here we put everyone else in danger?"

"You mean me," I say dully. "What if me being here puts everyone in danger."

"Well, I'm with Harper." Callie hasn't altered her position since this morning. "We stay and face whatever is coming, together. We fight."

"I'm not saying I don't want to fight." Jeremiah isn't defensive, though he was when Callie first said this. "I'm not afraid, Callie. I just think you don't know what it is we're facing, not really. Whereas Harper and I, we've seen it, up close. We've already fought Keziah off."

"But Harper isn't trying to go," Callie points out. "And it's her Keziah wants."

"What if Antoine is already under Keziah's control?" I say, again for probably the tenth time. "What if all this is a ruse to get us away from the mansion and the ground here? We don't know that my powers won't disappear away from here."

Jeremiah makes a frustrated noise and puts his head in his hands.

We're all tired. We've been having the same conversation for hours, and we're no closer to a resolution than we were at the start of it. The van Antoine bought is sitting out by the porch, white and unremarkable and so cold and empty it makes me want to cry. I can't imagine anything more lonely than packing boxes I've only recently unpacked into the back of it and driving off into an unknown future, with Callie and Jeremiah to look after. That thought makes me wonder if I'm being cowardly, and I feel confused all over again.

The sound of a truck approaching makes us all stiffen and my heart lurch with hope. But as it comes closer, I feel hope fade and tension take its place.

"It's Connor," I say, without getting up. The days when the thought of Connor brought hope are over. For a while now, I've tried to accept that my brother is gone. The hurt hasn't lessened, but I've discovered that the lack of hope makes disappointment easier to bear.

Callie, I realize, has gone very pale and turned away, so her face isn't easily visible from the door. For all her bravado, I know that Connor ignoring her presence here upsets her more than she lets on. I've caught her more than once peering into the room that used to be his, seeking to learn something, I guess, about the only brother she has.

Connor's tread is different than it used to be, less pronounced, as if he moves over the ground more easily. It's just another thing that reminds me that he is no longer my brother, but rather a supernatural creature. One I helped create, something I also find hard to forgive myself for, when I lie in bed at night and think of all we've lost, Callie and I.

"Harper?" He puts his head around the door before entering. It's an odd courtesy, one that reminds us all that he no longer lives here. It makes me sad.

"Connor." I say his name quietly and don't get up to greet him.

"Whose van is out front?"

"Ours, supposedly." I crumple one of the chip packets with unnecessary force. "Antoine brought it here," I say. "He wants us to take it and run. Leave Deepwater without telling anyone where we're going."

Connor's mouth twists. "Was that before or after Antoine went running off with Keziah?"

"Before." I put my hand up in a helpless gesture. "At least, we think it was."

"We're not sure," says Jeremiah. "That's the problem. Antoine might have already been under her control."

"Well, if he wasn't before, he certainly is now," Connor says grimly. "Both he and Cass have left the cabin. They're with Keziah now. The wolves tracked Keziah to the cabin. They had it surrounded, but I thought I could still talk Cass down. Then

Keziah did something, summoned her, I guess, and a moment later, both Antoine and Cass were gone."

"What about the wolves? Are they alright?"

Connor looks away at my question, and I see a shadow of something that might be guilt cross his face. "Henri was hurt," he says briefly.

"Remy's brother Henri? Badly?"

Connor shrugs dismissively, and when he turns back his face is hard again. "The wolves can take care of themselves," he says curtly. Not *ourselves*, I note. *So he doesn't see himself as one of them.* I don't know much about wolf packs, but something tells me that isn't good.

"I came to see if Antoine and Cass had been here," he says, looking at me. "But I see they haven't."

"No."

He nods then, as abruptly as he came, turns to go. I stand up. "Connor?" I can hear the pleading note in my voice. "Perhaps we could come back across the river with you. Help look for them. Do something, at least."

"You should take that van and go, Harper." He doesn't even turn around. Then Callie speaks.

"What if we went to the place you fought her last time? The place where you became a wolf?" Connor turns back and stares at her, as if he's seeing her for the first time. Callie meets his eyes steadily, though I can see the hectic points of color high on her cheeks. "Maybe if we go there, we can learn something about what this Caleb was, what Harper is. Work out a way to fight Keziah again."

"Why are you even still here?" Connor asks, and his tone is so cold I gasp. "You don't need to be anywhere near this. You should have left as soon as you got a look at this mess."

The sight of Callie's pinched face, sharp with hurt and shock, angers me more than I thought possible. I move so I'm hiding her from Connor. "I told you once before." My voice is low and fierce enough to take even me by surprise. "Callie is family, Connor. She stays."

Connor makes an impatient sound. "Do what you want," he says dismissively. "I honestly don't care, Harper. But stay away from the bayou. Stay on this side of the river. Over there is dangerous. It's no place for a couple of kids." He casts Jeremiah and Callie a contemptuous look that doesn't change when his eyes shift to me. "Nor for whatever it is that you are, Harper."

I've had enough. I move so fast I knock over a chair as I go. "I hate that you're like this," I say furiously. "I don't believe this is just *who you are now,* Connor, no matter what you say. I understand that you love Cass and miss her. I get it, believe me. But that doesn't give you the right to behave like this, to treat the rest of us as if we're nothing but an annoyance you don't have time for. If I want to go over the river and look at the ground there, then that is exactly what I'll do. And in the meantime, if you suddenly decide you need another potion to help out with your girlfriend or your wolves, good luck finding it. I'm not doing you any more favors."

He pauses at the door and stares at me, conflicting emotions shifting behind his eyes. "Don't cross the river, Harper," he says finally. "It isn't safe." His eyes cut briefly to Callie, but he says nothing more, just leaps off the porch. A moment later his truck takes off up the drive.

CHAPTER 10

ROSE

I drive the white van across the river still shaking with anger, my hands tight on the steering wheel. Whatever Connor has become, I've run out of patience with it. No matter how much I love him, I can't forgive his treatment of Callie. We've been through so much, he and I, fought to be a family when everyone, it seemed, wanted to tear us apart. We survived Mom's sickness and death when we were little more than children. We sat by Tessa's bedside, and then by her graveside. Through all that, Connor has been the one thing that was constant, the rock upon which I could rely. Even during all that's occurred since we came to Deepwater, I thought we'd find our way back to one another.

But where I could forgive the changes he was going through as a wolf, and as the partner of a vampire, I cannot forgive his bitterness toward Callie. It seems to hint at a part of him I never knew, a darkness in his character I hadn't glimpsed and feel no connection to. I don't want that version of Connor in my life. Every time I recall the hurt in Callie's eyes I feel a grim, hard anger I've never associated with Connor before. I'm disgusted that he could treat anyone as he has Callie, particularly someone who is actually family. I'm trying to push aside how I feel, but the anger lingers, making me fractious and off center.

The van is the only vehicle big enough to fit the three of us. It also offers an enclosed space to retreat to if we are attacked, something that feels like a safety net, though realistically I know that should Keziah decide to tear it apart, the metal wouldn't last a moment.

None of us speak. Callie hides whatever she is feeling by staring determinedly out the passenger window, but when Jeremiah's hand steals across to take hers, I notice she doesn't pull away. Her small hand curls into his, white and pale and oddly vulnerable.

I'm not sure if it's simply that the last memory I have of crossing the river is the night Connor was made, but something feels different the moment the van's wheels touch Louisiana ground. I feel the change like a thickening in atmosphere, as if the air is simply more dense here. I wind the window down and despite the rush of air, the night feels oppressive, lacking Mississippi's sultry movement. Stands of bayou cypress reach down into the still water, silent and ominous. We drive past the place where I turned my Mustang off the road months earlier, hiding it from Caleb's silent pursuit. My convertible has never quite recovered from that night. Every time I look at the dented undercarriage, I think of hiding in the growth, watching my brother transform.

I shake off the memory. If I could go back in time, I wonder, would I still agree to make the potion they used to turn Connor into what he is? It's just one more thing that feels like my fault, along with Keziah running loose, Cass being a vampire, and Remy's entire wolf pack struggling to come to terms with what they are.

"That's it." Jeremiah interrupts this unpleasant train of thought by pointing to the side road leading to the clearing. I take it, casting a wary eye around as we drive onto the wide ground, but I can't see past the dark trees surrounding it. Anything could be hidden behind them.

I sigh and park the van. There's no way of knowing what is out there. We may as well do what we came to.

"What are we looking for, exactly?" I ask Callie as we get out of the van.

"Anything that could help. Where is the place you fought off Caleb?"

I lead her across ground that feels strangely warm under my feet. Her hand is no longer in Jeremiah's, though she stays close to him, and when she thinks I'm not looking, I see her glance at him with the watchful, wary eyes of a wild animal. Where Avery drew a circle in salt around us, the grass is gone, the earth beneath burned a slightly darker shade. It's unsettling to see such visible evidence of what took place here. "This is Avery's salt circle." I lean down to touch it, and a faint shock runs up my arm.

"Where were you standing?" Callie is staring in fascination at the burned ground.

"Right opposite here." I move around the circle, oddly reluctant to enter it, until I'm standing in almost exactly the same place Caleb was when he faced me over the salt barrier. I brace, half expecting to feel him, but I don't. "Caleb was standing where I am now."

"Look." Callie points to the ground.

The ground spreading out from under my feet is marked like veins on an old man's hand, dark, gnarled lines that snake toward the salt circle. They are not raised from the ground, I realize, but rather the ground about them has eroded away, as if whatever runs through those veins is dark and toxic.

"And now look at where you were standing."

I follow Callie's gaze and clearly see the imprint of my feet, picked out now in deep crimson bayou rose. From the footprints, the roses trace lines similar in shape to the dark veins on this side of the circle, but as different as day from night. The bayou roses are rich and vibrant, lush lines of velvet flowers surrounded by emerald grass. At the salt circle they stop, abruptly, exactly where Caleb's dark counterparts meet them on the other side. It's like looking at a perfect mirror image where the form remains exactly the same, but the color and texture have been flipped. On Caleb's side, the veins are dark poison; on mine, flowery life.

"It's like a river," Callie says, leaning down to get a closer look, though I notice she doesn't touch either the bayou roses or the dark earth.

"Lori, Remy's mother, told me that water is a conduit for energy—and that the earth holds a lot of water." I stare at the veins branching across the ground. "That's the reason salt is traditionally used to block magic or energy."

"So y'all were fighting one another in the earth's water." Callie nods sagely, as if nothing about what she's just said is at all strange. "Makes sense." She stands up, brushing the dirt briskly from her hands.

"It does?" Jeremiah asks doubtfully. "How?"

"Because, dumbass," says Callie with exaggerated patience, "it's obvious, isn't it? Our girl Harper spreads life through the water. Y'all can see that plain as day at the mansion. While your boy here spreads death."

"Caleb," I say, somewhat unnecessarily. "His name was Caleb."

"Caleb, then." Callie nods at the dark lines. "Seems clear enough. An' he *was* dead, after all." She gives me a slightly uncomfortable look. "No offense to y'all."

"None taken." I'm still staring at the bayou roses. Even I can see how richly crimson they are, quite unlike anything I've seen before. "Caleb had the same ability as me," I say slowly. "Or something similar. Antoine told me that." I nod at the dark, poisonous lines. "I guess this is what it became after he was made a vampire."

A chill wind touches my back, a shadow rushing by me. For a moment I think it a memory. Then I feel a presence, cold and malign, and freeze.

"Harper!" Jeremiah's warning comes too late. I straighten up slowly, casting my eyes around.

A breath later, Keziah is standing before me. "It wasn't smart of you to come here all alone, Harper." Keziah's voice is low and velvety, like aged liquor, but her eyes gleam with preternatural savagery. I'm aware of Callie staring at her with fascination and, oddly, a complete absence of fear.

"You were talking about Caleb," she says conversationally, as if we were at a party and she had just accidentally overheard us. I wonder just how long she has been lurking in the woods, listening. "Your best guess cannot even begin to imagine the power Caleb had as vampire." Keziah is wearing a silk dress in deep purple, cut on a bias to show one gleaming shoulder and the dark depravity in her eyes. "Antoine is a fool," she says, her mouth twisting scornfully.

"What do you want, Keziah?" I'm proud that my voice is steady. "You've already taken Antoine and Cass. What more do you want?"

Keziah takes a step closer, her predatory eyes never leaving my face. "You know what I want," she says, in a low, intimate voice that curls around my insides like toxic smoke. "And tonight is where it begins." She moves so fast she is invisible. Before I can so much as think of defending myself, she holds me against her, my back to her chest, her grip so impossibly, unnaturally strong it's like being held by a machine, not a being. She has none of Antoine's glowing life. Her body is cold and unmoveable, like stone, and when she puts her cheek by mine it is not smooth marble but hard granite I sense, dead and unyielding. "Don't think of it," she says softly to Callie, as the thin figure starts toward her. "I will end you, little girl, if you take another step."

"Listen to her, Callie," I say in a choked voice. Keziah's arm is over my throat, cutting off my breath. I feel relieved when I see Jeremiah pull Callie back.

The arm that isn't gripping me comes up, and for a terrifying moment I think she will break my neck. Then I hear a sickening sound, like nails wrenched from wood, and realize in horror it is Keziah's teeth ripping into her own skin. A moment later she has thrust her arm into my mouth, and I am choking on the dark liquid that flows from it.

It isn't blood. Or it isn't anything like human blood. It seeps into my mouth in a cold, oily, insidious stream that seems to crawl down my throat, as if seeking its own path rather than waiting for me to swallow it. I choke and gag but Keziah's grip is like industrial steel, impersonal and effortless. "To become what he was, you need my blood inside you first." Her voice slides inside me with her blood. "You need to kill the part of you that would resist me. Become my creature before you die." The liquid falls from her arm until it is inside me whether I have swallowed or not. She holds me until I feel the dark stream begin to spread through my body. It feels as if she has held me forever and yet part of me is aware it has been no more than a second, not even long enough for Callie to cry out my name.

From a detached distance, I wonder how she intends to make me like Caleb, how it is done. Will I remember who I am now, I wonder, after I become whatever she intends to make me? Will I remember anything?

Then suddenly I'm free, falling to my knees. I gag, spitting her blood to the ground. Keziah is crouched, snarling, facing a group of figures I can't quite make out, focused as I am on ridding my body of the poison I can feel spreading through it.

"You can't fight all of us, Keziah." It's Tate's voice, calm and steady, and I feel a surge of relief so passionate it almost blocks out the sickening taste in my mouth. Blearily, I look across the clearing and realize Connor is there, in wolf form, with Remy at his side. A pale-faced Avery stands behind them.

Keziah puts a cold hand on my neck, holding me down.

"You can't turn Harper," Tate goes on. "Not with us here, Keziah. You will be too weak to fight us if you do. Leave, or die as soon as you do it."

"You can't," Keziah hisses. Her hand clenches on my skin, fingers of steel digging into my flesh.

"I think we can." Tate takes a step closer, the wolves growling at his side, bronze eyes glowing in the night. "And I think that without Caleb to bring you back, this time you will simply be dead, Keziah. Let Harper go."

Keziah's hand tightens again. The wolves crouch low to the ground, snarling, and I realize it is a stand off. The wolves will not attack while she holds me hostage, and Keziah will not risk her life by letting me go. She leans close to me. "I have Antoine," she says in a low voice that nonetheless carries across the clearing. "And I have Cass." The black wolf that is Connor snarls savagely, claws digging into the soil. "They belong to me now," Keziah goes on, and I can hear the triumph in her voice. "They are my children, a bond greater than even you wolves can understand. I have called them home to my side, and they are under my command. Should I fall here, tonight, they will not be freed of that bond. They will take revenge for my death, and then they will turn on one another." Connor howls, a high, sharp sound of anguish, as the impact of her words sinks into us all. "If you follow me," Keziah goes on, "Antoine and Cass will die. I swear it to you." She eyes them across the clearing. "And this one," she says, shaking me once, scornfully, before throwing me facedown into the soil, "now she, too, is marked by my blood. She will be another of my children. The most powerful, I think, of them all." She kicks me so I roll over, facing her gleaming eyes and cold, inhuman expression. She puts her face close to mine.

"I will come back for you," she hisses, stroking my face with one long finger. "And when I do, Harper, you will never leave my side again."

Then she is gone, no more than stale smoke on the night air, the wolves howling in her wake.

CHAPTER 11

TAÍNO

Keziah's blood tastes like death on my tongue, like ash and cold fire. I retch and swill my mouth with water from the bottle Jeremiah hands me, but I can still feel her poison spreading through me, like Caleb's dark veins on the earth. In my mind, I can see Keziah's essence crawling through my blood, predatory and exultant, seeking to make what I am into her creature. I want to scratch the inside of my veins, claw her out of my body. Her presence inside me is the darkest, most insidious sensation I have ever experienced, a cancer that makes my body a stranger and makes me in turn more afraid and angry than I've ever been.

Connor and Remy race after Keziah, but they return in minutes, having taken human form. "She's gone," Connor says curtly. His face is dark and twisted and he barely casts me a glance. Remy looks older than I remember. When Avery runs to him, he pulls her close, kissing the top of her head and murmuring reassurance to her in a way that makes me sad and lonely.

"How are you?" Tate kneels beside me, putting his hand on my shoulder.

"I've felt better." I wipe my mouth and sit shakily back on the ground, my arms on my knees. I don't trust my legs to stand. "Where were you, Tate? I've tried to call, email. Antoine, too. You didn't answer any of us." A fleeting look of something like guilt passes over Tate's face.

"I'm sorry about that," he says. "I wasn't sure what to say."

"'I'm alive' would have been a good beginning," I say wryly. It's hard to remain angry with Tate. Diplomacy is a gift he was born with, one that was only made stronger after he became a vampire. Just as Antoine carries the power of the medicine woman who sacrificed herself for him, Tate carries the nature of the savage soldier he took into himself. It seems strange to me sometimes that the gift Tate took from the white soldier's death was not the man's murderous nature, but rather an understanding of the mindset behind the killer and a comprehension of white history and thought. Perhaps it is simply the nearness of my own transformation at Keziah's hands, the awareness that I, too, may very soon need to face such conflict, that makes me think of this now. Whatever the reason, I'm suddenly very much in awe of what it must have taken for Tate to not only understand the man whose nature became part of his own, but to seek to express that nature in a positive, rather than negative, way.

"I should have answered your calls, I know." Tate's voice brings me back to my surroundings. "And part of me expected Antoine to summon me. I couldn't have fought it, if he had."

"But he didn't."

"No, Harper." Tate's voice is full of a compassion that hurts almost as much as Keziah's blood in my veins. "He didn't."

Callie and Jeremiah stand a few feet away, watching me anxiously. Avery and Remy are still absorbed in one another, and I notice Jeremiah looking uncomfortably away from them. Connor stands at a slight distance from us all, looking into the trees, as if seeking a glimpse of Cass.

I could tell him he won't find her. I can feel that Keziah is gone, and that Cass and Antoine are out of reach, at least for now.

"Let's go home." Tate offers me his arm, helping me up.

"We're coming with you." Connor addresses Tate, not me. "Whatever information you bring, the wolves need it too."

Remy frowns. "I'm not sure that's a good idea."

"Then don't come." Connor's words come out as a vicious snarl, and Remy bites off whatever he was going to say, though by the resentful look in his eyes, I can tell it hurts him to do so. Nonetheless, he follows Connor, his shoulders hunched and resigned, Avery close to his side.

Tate drives the van, Jeremiah beside him. I sit in the back with Callie, welcoming the darkness and her tactful silence. Callie, I am realizing, possesses the rare skill of being in a place without occupying it. Her presence is somehow soothing. For much of the journey home, I fight nausea and sheer, splintering terror, alongside a crippling feeling of inadequacy. After all my time training with Callie, in the end I was no more effective against Keziah than a bug against a windshield. I couldn't have fought her no matter what I did. The thought is unutterably depressing. I've never considered myself a victim. But it's hard to feel like anything else when I'm up against something with the strength of steel and blood that poisons my own.

When we reach the Mississippi side of the river, I feel sweet relief in the cool river breeze and the scent of magnolias. I wonder if this is how Connor and the wolves feel on the other side of the river. I wind down the window and inhale the sweet night breeze, my heart filling as we turn through the gates of the mansion.

I'm home, Tessa, I think, mentally reaching for the earth in which the last of my sister's ashes lie. *We're safe again.* It's only when I see Callie looking at me strangely that I realize I've whispered the words aloud.

Tate helps me inside, and by the time I'm seated at the kitchen table, drinking an extremely strong rum concoction of Callie's creation, Connor's truck pulls up outside. He, Remy, and Avery enter without speaking and stand by the door, arms folded and faces forbidding, looking for all the world like grim judges about to pronounce a sentence.

"Speak," says Connor to Tate. His eyes pass over Callie but don't pause. He doesn't even look at me. I wish it didn't hurt so much to see how much he doesn't care.

Tate's eyes narrow slightly. He takes his time, pouring himself a drink, offering one to both Callie and Jeremiah with an almost exaggerated courtesy, ignoring Connor's glowering expression. Finally he takes his seat, folds his legs elegantly, takes a sip of his drink, and begins.

"Some time ago, during a class on slavery, one of my students came across a mention of the Taíno people, the indigenous inhabitants of Haiti. I didn't think much of it at the time, except that it might be an interesting topic for them to pursue. Then I began to do some research of my own and realized the student might have stumbled across something important. Shortly after that, the student came back with a story relating to Taíno mythology—and I knew without a doubt that we had something."

His eyes flicker to me. "Jared," I say. "I remember the article. Something about a god who guarded a cave."

Tate nods. "It triggered a memory of a story I heard long ago, from another of our kind who had an interest in the area, and I decided to go and investigate in person. I reached out to a professional contact, the author of the paper Jared had read. Daniel is a lecturer in Caribbean culture at the university in Port-au-Prince in Haiti. His own ancestry is Taíno. He offered to share the resources of the university with me as a professional courtesy, and I flew out the same day." Tate speaks directly to me, and I nod, remembering the day he left. "I wasn't entirely sure what I was looking for, but after a few days I real-ized I wouldn't learn anything at the university in Port-au-Prince. The knowledge I needed wasn't academic. It was tribal, the mythology no native people share willingly with white men. I asked Daniel if he'd show me some of the places mentioned in his papers. He said yes, of course. As one indigenous person to another." A shadow crosses his face. "As soon as we left the city, I compelled him to take me to the places sacred to his people, places I knew he wouldn't have written about."

I can tell he loathed having done this to Daniel. Deception, I know, doesn't come easily to Tate, even if he first came to Deep-water under false pretenses.

"Daniel took me to a place far from the city, deep in the mountains, near a waterfall. There was a cave inside the moun-tain, but he was clearly afraid to go anywhere near it. The cave, he said, was once—many, many millennia ago—the shelter of people known to the Taíno as 'stone people.' Feared creatures, that only came out at night."

"Vampires," I breathe.

Tate nods. "According to Daniel, one of the Taíno was appointed to be sentinel for the stone people. Macocael, as he was known in their language. This sentinel, Macocael, had special powers that helped him resist the calls of the stone people. It was his job to ensure they remained safely in the mountain cave."

"Compulsion," I say. "He couldn't be compelled, like me."

"It seems so," says Tate. "But according to the story Daniel told, one night, for reasons lost to time, Macocael left his post. When he did, the creatures inside the cave escaped. Macocael himself was 'turned to stone.'" Tate looks around at us. "I think we can assume that means he was made vampire.

"Daniel took me then to the nearby waterfall, a place so sacred to Haitians that he would not allow me to touch the water, though I believe his own people make pilgrimage there.

At the time of the stone people, he said, it had been the place of a goddess named Abatey, who ruled both water and fertility."

His eyes rest briefly on me then shift away.

"The Taíno believed that while Abatey lived in the water and could not be seen, she was physically embodied, in every generation, in the form of a young Taíno woman. The Taíno worshipped these young women, who were always immediately recognizable as embodiments of Abatey because of their special gifts with earth and water." Tate glances at me again. Jeremiah shifts uncomfortably, and Avery folds her arms, as if this piece of information somehow annoys her.

"According to myth," Tate says, and I'm aware of how he continually emphasizes the mythological nature of his tale, as if to separate it from our current reality, "Macocael had to kill one of the Taíno in order to become as the other stone people were. He killed the girl who embodied Abatey—by draining her of her blood."

The night feels suddenly hushed. Nobody moves or speaks, our attention focused only on Tate and his story.

"Drinking the human embodiment of Abatey gave Macocael access to the terrible power of the water and fertility goddess. But he himself had already been contaminated by the stone people, and so when he drained the young girl, the power of the goddess twisted in his system. He could access the power of water, it was true, follow it through earth or any other physical form in which water was contained. But where Abatey and her embodiments spread life through soil and water, Macocael instead—"

"Spread death," I finish his sentence. "He spread the power of death, not life."

Tate nods slowly. "Blood, remember, is a form of water. Macocael could spread death through blood. But in those who were already dead, his power was reversed. He could rejuvenate them, using the power of Abatey he now held.

"For the Taíno, of course, this was terrifying. Now there was no way to kill the stone creatures. Even if they burned in the sun, Macocael could rejuvenate them, so that the following night, they would appear as if they had never died."

"How did it end?" It is Callie who asks. "What happened to all the stone people?"

"Daniel knew nothing of their end. They seem to fade from mythology. Whether they left for other places, or ran out of blood to feed upon—who knows? They are not mentioned again. All that is left to us is the tale of Macocael's transformation, and the moral tale of him leaving his post, an error that is always blamed on him being seduced—by a very beautiful woman."

"Keziah," I say flatly.

Tate nods.

"And this sentinel, Macocael. He was Caleb?"

"We can assume that, I think, yes. It seems a natural enough change of name, from a pagan tradition to one more in line with Abrahamic religions and western culture."

"How old are they, then? You said 'many millennia.' Just how many did you mean?"

"Some scholars believe the Taíno came from the deep Amazon. Others believe their origins lay in the mountains of the Andes. Either way, by the time of European colonization in the fifteenth century, the Taíno had existed in the Caribbean as a complex culture for at least two thousand years, and in the Amazon or Andes for much longer before that." Tate looks at me soberly. "It's highly possible that the story of the stone people in fact describes a conflict between these two tribes— those of the Amazon and uof the Andes."

I think back to Keziah's iron grip. "That's what Keziah felt like to me," I say quietly. "Granite, stone. Something profoundly different from you or Antoine. There's nothing human in her form. It's cold and hard, utterly dead."

Tate nods. "And for centuries, now, if not millennia, she has been rejuvenated by the power of death itself. Whatever Keziah may once have been, she is now dead a thousand times over. Caleb's power of death is the only thing coursing through her body."

"And now in mine." I shudder, fighting the urge to claw at my skin. "I can feel her, Tate. Keziah. Inside me."

"That's why she wants you." It's Callie who speaks, her piercing blue eyes watching me closely. "You're one of those Abatey girls, Harper. Keziah wants to make you into another Caleb, so she can be alive. Or—not dead." She shrugs impatiently. "Whatever Keziah is."

"Then why didn't she?" Remy asks, frowning. "If she wanted to make you her little goddess of death, why didn't Keziah just take you then and there? Why capture you and let you go again?"

"Because you were there," I say, confused. "The wolves and Tate. She knew she couldn't beat you." I would have thought that was obvious.

"No." Connor's voice is gravelly and tired, and he seems to speak almost reluctantly. "Remy's right. She's fought us off before, and she could certainly outrun us. She wanted you to drink her blood, but she let you go." He looks directly at me for the first time that night. "We need to know why she did that, Harper. What Keziah might be afraid of."

CHAPTER 12

TRUCE

In the awkward silence that follows, Tate stands up.

"Where are you going?" I try to hide the fear in my voice. I don't want Tate to go. He feels like my only connection to the Antoine I know, the only thing holding together this strange alliance of Connor, Remy, and Avery. I'm afraid that when he leaves, they will too. The thought of being without him leaves me cold and bereft.

"I need to find Antoine." Tate looks at me apologetically.

"Then I'm coming with you." Connor peels away from the doorframe.

"No." Tate's voice is calm, but commanding nonetheless. Connor's eyes narrow. "If Antoine senses you nearby, at best, he will run," Tate says. "At worst, he'll kill you." He meets Connor's skeptical gaze. "Don't think he won't," he says quietly. "You forget that I know Antoine in this state. I've seen it before. He's ruthless and utterly lethal. Hunting and killing was once what Antoine did best. Under Keziah's control, he applied those skills with deadly accuracy. None could stand before him. You certainly won't."

"And what makes you so sure he won't kill you?" Connor counters.

Tate gives him a wan smile. "I'm not at all sure he won't try." Deep in his soft brown eyes a strange, violet light shimmers. "Though it must be said that I am not without my own talents, when it comes to killing."

Connor's face hardens into an expression of disgust that seems to bother Tate not at all. He smiles blandly. "I will assume your silence means you won't try to follow me, Connor. I would certainly advise against it." He doesn't wait for a response, just presses my hand reassuringly, and murmurs that he will see me soon. He nods at Jeremiah and Callie, touches Avery on the shoulder, and is gone with the unsettling swiftness of his kind, leaving behind an awkward, charged silence.

For a while nobody moves or says anything. Then Remy goes to the refrigerator. "If we're temporarily calling a truce"—he smiles at me with a tired hint of his old bravado—"the least you can do is let me drink your beer."

I shrug. "Help yourself. It's Connor's, anyway." Remy cracks the top from one and throws another to Connor, who catches it without showing any reaction. His face hasn't lightened in the least from the start of Tate's story to the end. I notice that Remy leaves a wary distance between them as he returns to Avery's side.

"If Keziah didn't take you, Harper," Jeremiah says, frowning, "it means there's something about you that isn't safe for her. What would it be?"

I shake my head. "I have no idea. Whatever power I have is useless against her. When she came for me, I couldn't so much as think about trying to access it, let alone somehow fight her off with it. I've never felt so powerless in my life as I did when she was feeding me her blood. The only other time I've felt so helpless was when Tessa—" The words are out before I can stop them, and they hang awkwardly in the air. I can't look at

Connor. He knows I was about to say *when Tessa was dying*. It feels wrong, though, to talk about my twin now, when all that remains of the family she knew and loved is so badly fractured. For all my concern, though, Connor seems to have barely registered my slip, and that makes me even sadder.

"It isn't you fighting her that Keziah is afraid of," says Callie. When we all turn to her, she rolls her eyes impatiently. "Well, it's obvious, ain't it?" Her accent has thickened, as it always does when she's self-conscious. "It's your blood Keziah's afraid of."

For a moment I hesitate, remembering what Antoine said, his warning not to share what he suspected about Keziah. Then I think of Antoine at Keziah's side, her slave once more, and think of all that is at risk because of me, and suddenly I don't care what danger it puts me in anymore.

"Antoine said as much," I say hesitantly, glancing briefly at Connor, who for once is actually looking at me. "He said that my blood has powers that Keziah understands."

Connor leans slightly forward. "But if your blood has power," he says, frowning, "isn't that more reason to drink it?"

I try not to let the hurt show in my eyes when they meet his. "Cass didn't," I say quietly.

His mouth closes as effectively as if I've struck him. Suddenly tired of the charade, I push on.

"The night we got Cass back, you told me that she *had enough to worry about, without trying not to drink my blood*. What did you mean by that?"

Watching my brother's face, I can see him struggle with the same choice I just made, between keeping Cass's secrets and trying to solve the problem we face.

"It's you who said we should share information. If you know something, Connor, you should at least share it."

"Fine." Connor takes a long pull on his beer, his face hard and unfriendly as he looks at me. "Cass said she'd never tasted anything like your blood, Harper. She said it made her feel—the most alive she had since she became a vampire."

"Antoine said the same." But there's something in Connor's face, an odd kind of light, that makes me think there is more to what he said that I don't know—and that he has no intention of telling me.

"Well, there you are." Callie looks between us. "We know what it is that she's afraid of, then. Your blood can make a vampire human."

"And if they're human," says Remy, looking at me curiously, "that means we can kill them." His eyes cut to Connor and slide away again, and suddenly I realize why Connor has been so hell-bent on keeping me away from Cass—and keeping my powers a secret.

"We don't know that," I say hastily.

"But it's a fair assumption." Jeremiah is frowning, deep in thought. "I think there's more to it, though."

"Like what?" Connor's face is dark as a winter storm.

"Well, if the only issue is that Harper can make her feel alive, Keziah could still have taken her, couldn't she? It wouldn't have been hard. I think it's more than that."

Callie speaks up, looking at Jeremiah. "To be made a vampire, a person has to be completely drained of their blood, right?"

Jeremiah nods.

"Then Keziah wants someone else to drain Harper," Callie says. Jeremiah nods again. "Well, then? Who?"

"Not Antoine." Jeremiah looks at her as if they communicate in their own private shorthand. They remind me of a little of a pair of private detectives, welding together their case. "Keziah needs him for protection."

"Cass, then." Callie frowns. "But why?"

"Harper's blood cuts through their vampire powers," Jeremiah says slowly. "Which means that if Antoine or Cass drains her, Keziah will lose control over them."

"Which means they will try to stop her hurting Harper." Now Callie is nodding. "So she needs one to remain under her control to protect her from that— and possibly kill the other one, if needed."

"Cass can't kill Antoine." Connor interrupts them, his voice tense with fear. "She's told me that. It's something to do with him putting the mark on her body and the fact that he is older than her. She told me Antoine is stronger than her, much stronger. He always will be. He can't command her, exactly, but next to Keziah, it's Antoine who has the most ability to influence her."

"Then she's keeping Antoine safe so he can kill Cass."

Avery says what none of the rest of us want to, and her words fall into the kitchen with cold clarity. Nobody is looking directly at me, but once again, I can feel their collective hostility, the unspoken belief that all of this comes down to me, is my fault. I take a deep breath.

"There is another option," I say quietly.

"What?" Connor's eyes on me are hard and accusing. I glance between Callie and Jeremiah, who are watching me expectantly. I know they have left this up to me, whether to tell the others everything I know or not.

"We somehow get hold of Antoine's blood," I say. "And activate whatever power is inside me."

"What do you mean, *activate* it?"

I meet my brother's hard stare with one of my own. "Antoine's blood has power of its own. From the medicine woman he drank when he was made. It's why he could make the sun totem on Cass's skin." I take a step toward Connor. "And how he could make you what you are." I don't say the word wolf, and when I see Remy's dangerous expression, I'm glad I didn't. Remy doesn't like what my brother is, I realize, nor how

Connor came to be wolf. Not at all. He resents Connor's power over him.

"So if you drink Antoine's blood," Connor says slowly, "it could activate you in some way? Like what? What will you become?"

"That's just it," says Callie, her eyes bright and hard as she looks at Connor. "Nobody knows what Harper will become. Which is exactly why Antoine refused to do it in the first place, and why he wants Harper far away from here. Especially now that she has Keziah's blood in her veins."

Shaking off Remy's arm, Avery steps forward, glaring at me.

"Of course, it's all about you," she snaps. "Never mind the fact that Cass is gone. Or that bayou people—*our* people, Harper—are being killed every night to satisfy Keziah's bloodlust and the insanity of the vampires under her control. Never mind the fact that your brother has taken over a wolf pack he has no natural right to rule, or that Cass's mother was murdered in cold blood, and nobody even knows. No. Just so long as you're kept safe, it doesn't seem to matter who else has to be sacrificed." Her eyes glitter with anger. "Well, I say if there's something you can actually do to stop all this, then at the very least, you owe it to us to try."

A cold feeling spreads through my stomach. I can't argue with Avery. I don't even want to.

Callie leaps to her feet, eyes flashing fiercely. "And what happens if Harper becomes something like this Caleb creature was, something dead and evil, capable of killing us all? What if she becomes something none of us even recognize? If she herself is lost forever? Are you going to be okay with that too, Avery?" She turns to Connor. "Are *you* going to be alright with that?"

Connor, though, doesn't answer. And after a brief, charged silence, I put a hand on Callie's arm, and reluctantly she sits down again.

"It's my choice, Callie," I say quietly. "And this is what I want to do." I look around the room, at Remy and Connor. "Can you do it?" I ask them. "Can you hunt Antoine down for long enough to get some of his blood?"

"Wait a minute," says Jeremiah, looking about warily. "Shouldn't we at least talk to Tate about this? Ask him to help?"

"You heard what he said." Connor's eyes glitter dangerously. "He won't help us, not with this. He thinks Antoine is too strong."

Callie stares right back at him. "And what if he's right?"

"We can bring Antoine down," says Connor grimly. "We'll get that blood."

"You're just saying that because you want Cass back." Avery glares at him.

"I thought you were the one saying Harper owed it to us?" Connor throws back at her.

"That was before I realized you were going to use the wolves to do it." Avery shakes her head. "You don't care about anything except Cass, Connor. Can't you see how that has changed you? Don't you care at all about the pack you lead?"

Connor rounds on her, looming over Avery's slender figure and almost snarling at Remy when the other moves to interfere. "I care about nothing," he hisses, right in her face. "Nothing, do you understand? Nothing, except getting Cass back, and keeping her safe. And if you're smart"—he glares around the room at each of us in turn—"you would all do well to remember that."

CHAPTER 13

ALPHA

A tense standoff is broken by Remy muttering that he is going to contact the wolves and stalking outside with his phone, closely followed by Avery. The rest of us look awkwardly at each other, trying not to look at Connor, who is staring moodily out the door. "Well?" he says, as Remy and Avery come back inside.

"They'll do it." Remy and Avery exchange a glance.

"What?" demands Connor.

It's Avery, rather than Remy, who faces my brother. "This is the last time," she says. Her face is unusually determined. "The wolves will do this, because they know what Cass means to you, and because it's Remy asking. But you have to know they've reached their limit."

"What do you mean?" I ask when Connor doesn't respond. "What limit?"

"Being near vampires is torture for wolves." Avery glances at Connor. "*Normal* wolves," she amends, and a dark flush rises on Connor's neck. Despite the distance between us, I sense his hurt and feel an unexpected sympathy for him. "Having Cass live in the bayou has been difficult," Avery goes on. "The wolves have tolerated it because of Connor. But that ends now, tonight."

"Avery." Remy throws her a warning glance and steps forward, meeting Connor's eyes. "She's right," he says quietly. "I wish it weren't this way, brother. I do. But it is what it is. If I call on the pack one more time in Cass's name, they'll tear us both apart, especially if it means they have to watch while your girl-friend tears their own people apart."

"And you?" Connor's voice isn't angry. It's more resigned, as if he's seen this coming for a while—which, if what Avery told me weeks ago is true, he probably has.

"I'm done too, Connor." Remy meets his eyes steadily. "A pack can't have two alphas, brother. And I can't bow to you anymore, even if it means my death. Not if it means standing by why my own people suffer."

Connor nods slowly. "After this is done, I'll leave the bayou. Cass and I won't bother you again." He steps forward and puts out his hand to Remy. "I'll make sure it doesn't come to a fight," he says. "They're your pack, Remy. I'll make sure they all know that." Remy takes his hand in a hard, tight grip.

"I'll be sorry to see you go," he says roughly, and I can tell he means it. Then the words sink in.

"Wait," I say, turning to Connor. "Go? Where are you going to go?"

"I don't know yet." Connor doesn't look at me. "This isn't the time for it, Harper."

I'm about to argue that this is precisely the time, when I catch sight of Avery's face and subside. Callie covers my hand with her own. Remy glances at me. "We're not going after Antoine tonight," he says. Connor is already edging out the door. "Tate might be with him, and we can't risk fighting both of them." The thought of my brother pitted against Tate and Antoine gives me a hollow feeling inside, and all I can do is nod.

"We'll call tomorrow," Avery says, as all three of them head out to their vehicles, parked haphazardly beneath the oak out front. "Tell you what's happening."

"Thanks." Callie's voice behind me is loaded with sarcasm, but it's wasted on Avery, who has already turned her back. We stand on the porch until the vehicles are gone, then go indoors, night closing about us.

Callie, Jeremiah, and I sit in the kitchen, looking at each other. "Are you alright?" Callie asks gently, covering my hand with her own. "Does it hurt? Keziah's blood?"

"It doesn't hurt, exactly." I take a gulp of Callie's rum concoction, welcoming the alcohol inside me in a way I never have before, wanting to drown out the feeling of Keziah's presence. "It's more as if I can sense her, as if part of her is alive in my mind. It's a little like when I first moved here, when she was still bound in the cellar, and I would dream of her whispering to me. Only this is worse. It's a feeling, rather than a voice I hear. It's almost as if part of me *is* her. Or becoming her." I drink again. "It's awful," I say flatly, facing Callie and Jeremiah. "And if it's like that for me, I can't even imagine what it must be like for Cass and Antoine."

We talk for a while, speculating about what is happening across the bayou, how the wolves might go about trying to capture Antoine, but none of us really knows anything. In the end, Jeremiah and I drink most of the bottle of rum between us, Callie mixing the drinks quietly but not touching them herself. "Seen enough of bottles with my momma," she says briefly when I ask if she wants a drink. "Don't need it." She sees my face and gives me a small smile. "No judgment," she says. "Anyone could do with a drink tonight, it's y'all."

But the booze doesn't seem to help, and as the sun rises, I fall into bed feeling as sober as I did before I had the first drink.

~

I SLEEP MOST OF THE DAY AWAY, AND THE SHADOWS ARE LONG when I wake. I squint at the sun, wondering why it makes me feel mildly sick, then remember Keziah's blood coursing through my veins and stumble to the bathroom. Staring at myself in the mirror, I wonder if my hair isn't just a little duller than I recall, the wild mass of curls a little flatter. *Is she killing me slowly, from the inside out?* I wonder. *Is it different for people like me than for normal humans?*

But I can't know the answers, and I'm not sure I want to. I shower and dress and come downstairs to find Callie and Jeremiah already in the kitchen. I get the feeling I've interrupted a conversation. I take the coffee Callie hands me and look between them. "What's happened?"

They look at each other, then at me. Callie answers. "Avery called. The wolves are heading off now. They think they know where to find Antoine."

I look out the window. Darkness is falling, though the moon is not yet visible. Somewhere out there, I think, my brother, Remy, and the wolves are racing to what might be their deaths. To take blood from my husband, who may himself die.

The thought makes me feel sicker than I did when I woke. "Has Tate called?"

Their silence is answer enough.

Unable to be inside any longer, I head out onto the back porch with my coffee and walk barefoot through the damp grass toward the river. I need the feel of the earth under my feet, the smell of the river close by, and magnolias on the air. I need to be feeling anything other than the stagnant atmosphere of waiting for news that, no matter how I imagine it, can't be good. I wonder how the pack plans to take Antoine's blood while they are in wolf form, but we already wasted hours speculating last night, and I don't fancy going over it again.

I'm standing on the jetty, looking moodily out over the water, when something stirs the darkness. I narrow my eyes and glance about warily, relaxing when I see Callie and Jeremiah. "You shouldn't come up on me like that," I say a little sharply. "You scared me." Then they come closer, and I see their pale, frightened expressions. Jeremiah holds up his phone.

"It's Avery." Callie stares warily about her. "She thinks Keziah might be headed here. She told us to go back across the river, to the clearing. She'll meet us there."

"But I'm stronger here." I shake my head, remembering the last time I fled the mansion. "How do we know it isn't a trick?"

"We don't," says Jeremiah. He holds out his cellphone. Avery's name is on the screen.

"Hello?" I say uncertainly.

"Harper." There's no mistaking the urgency in Avery's voice. "You need to get out of there, now. Please trust me."

"I do trust you." My eyes search the shadows for movement. "But I don't feel strong on that side of the river, Avery. I'm better here."

"The wolves have lost Keziah. They think she's headed your way."

Cold dread grips me. We can't fight Keziah if she compels Cass or Antoine to drain me. I try to shake the thoughts, to ignore the oily sensation of her blood in my body.

"Have you seen Tate?"

There's a pause that doesn't leave me feeling reassured, then Avery says roughly, "The wolves think Tate might be lost. The Marigny ground might be your ground, Harper, but the clearing over the river is mine. I can protect you better here than I can there. I'm your best chance." She pauses. When I don't answer, she says, "I'm sorry to say it like this, Harper. But I might also be your only chance."

I hand the phone back to Jeremiah. "Let's go," I say dully.

CHAPTER 14

DEAD

*J*eremiah drives, Callie at his side. It's my turn to stare out the window, wondering what awaits us on the other side of the slow, thick water below. Never have the bayous felt more sinister, more hushed and silent, as if just waiting for me to walk into their steamy depths and be sucked from existence.

Avery is alone in the clearing when we arrive. We park on the edge and walk cautiously to where she stands. "Get inside the circle I made last time," she says by way of greeting. "I'll make a salt barrier like I did then."

"Where are the wolves?"

"Chasing them," she answers briefly. She doesn't meet my eyes. I know *them* means Cass and Antoine. I just can't imagine how we got to a place where it is *us* and *them*, with the man I love and the girl my brother loves on the other side of the salt circle.

"I can't fight him, Avery," I say quietly. "If it comes to it. I just don't think I can."

"I think we're about to find out," says Callie, in small, slightly unsteady voice. "They're here."

"What do you mean?" I spin around, peering into the darkness. "Who's here?" But my question is moot. Emerging from the darkness, silent as shadows and just as expressionless, are Cass and Antoine.

"Where are the wolves?" Jeremiah hisses.

Avery shakes her head, watching warily as the two vampires approach. "I don't know."

"They've gone after Keziah." I spin around. It's Connor, clad in nothing more than torn shorts, still covered in dirt from his recent transformation. "I asked Remy to let me try to speak to Cass." His eyes slide to me and it hurts to see the agony in them. "I have to try, Harper." I nod. I understand.

Cass and Antoine are close now, barely twenty yards away, outside Avery's old salt circle. She hasn't tried to make a new one after all. I think, somehow, she knows salt won't work. How can it, when what Connor and I want is on the outside of the circle, rather than inside it? Something tells me magic can't work like that, against the heart.

"Antoine." I reach out my hand. Antoine doesn't move. His eyes are dark and flat, neither with none of the storm tossed complexity I've come to love, the turbulent palette of cobalt, slate and gold that shifts like a tropical sky. Instead they are just empty, like stagnant water in which nothing lives.

"Keziah fed me her blood, Antoine."

Not by so much as a flicker does his expression change. It's unnerving, like looking at a wax figure.

"She's going to kill me," I go on, trying to keep the panic from my voice. "Make me her servant, as she did Caleb. My only chance for survival is if you give me your blood."

Still nothing. I hold up my hand, so the emerald gleams in the moonlight.

"*Always*, Antoine. You said we would face everything together, always. Remember?"

"Harper," Jeremiah says quietly. "He's not wearing his ring." I glance at Antoine's hand and cold grips my heart. His finger is bare, the wedding ring he swore never to take off, gone. Somehow that, more than his blank eyes and silence, is the thing that breaks me.

"He's gone," I whisper, staring at Antoine's blank face, which doesn't so much as register my words. "Antoine is gone."

"Cass!" Connor calls hoarsely. "If you don't come back to me now, the wolves will kill you. I can't hold them anymore. They're coming, Cass. Please." His voice breaks on the last word, and I can hear my own heartbreak echoed in my brother's voice.

"She can't."

Keziah's high, clear voice cuts across the clearing like a knife. She is standing to our left, on Cass's right-hand side. Despite her standing some distance away, I see Cass tremble, swaying slightly toward Keziah, as if the particles of her body are drawn to her ancient Maker. "Cass is my child." Keziah smiles coldly. "Neither she nor Antoine can defy me forever. It is natural law that they submit to me."

"Antoine." Ignoring her, I say his name again, even though I know it's futile. "I know you're in there. Remember Tate? You made him, Antoine. He's still out there somewhere, searching for you—"

"No, he isn't." Keziah's mouth stretches in a cold smile that has nothing to do with the venal darkness of her eyes. "I ordered Antoine to kill his progeny. Tell her, Antoine." Her command, given carelessly, without so much as glancing at Antoine, is chilling.

"Tate is dead."

Antoine's response is as emotionless as his face, delivered with cold, hard finality.

Dead.

Not gone, or finished, or any other word that may leave room for hope.

Just *dead,* taking the last shred of hope I had and throwing it into the sucking swamp of the bayou. I stiffen. It will be a fight, then.

The wolves slink among the trees behind Antoine, bellies low to the ground, keeping a wary distance as they circle the three vampires. One of them darts in suddenly, coming for Keziah. A moment later, so fast I don't see the movement, the wolf is flying through the air, yelping in pain as it hits a tree. Keziah seems not to have moved at all. She is still smiling. "You should call off your dogs," she says to Connor. "They will die here tonight."

Without waiting for an answer, she turns to Cass, who slowly swivels to face her. *As if Cass is a puppet on a string,* I think, *to be tugged this way or that, utterly without thought.*

"Cass," says Keziah in a conversational tone. "Drain Harper."

There isn't time for fear. There's no time at all between Keziah's command and Cass's preternatural rush. I hear the words and then there is only Cass's iron grip and the sharp, piercing agony of her teeth sinking into my neck.

It isn't like it was the time Antoine drank from me, long ago, in the tunnels. That was a sensual river in which I was him and he was me, a tidal rush I wanted never to end. This is entirely different, though just as consuming, albeit in a dark, terrifying way.

Her teeth sink into my flesh and the rest of the world disappears, taking time with it, so there is only her deep penetration of my body and my blood rushing into her hungry mouth. I can no longer hear nor see; I have no awareness of anything other than the connection between Cass and me. It is a ruthless siphoning of my life and all that I am, taking without mercy, as if the very essence of my soul is being stripped from my veins, leaving nothing but a dried, paper-thin husk. I do not know how long it goes on, only that I feel it, the moment when the last fragile piece of moisture in my body is about to flee, and with it my life; then I am dropped unceremoniously to the ground.

Shouts penetrate my stupor. I am once more aware of a world beyond blood and death. I can hear Connor yelling, Callie's screams. My eyelids flutter, the effort to open them seeming too much, but Connor's roar tugs something visceral within me that forces them up, the warm air fiery agony on my dried eyes.

Keziah is standing over me, eyes gleaming, her arm raised to her mouth. She's about to feed me, then break my neck. I don't know how I know it, only that I do. It's this moment she has come for. It's her blood that lines the husk of my body, the only force keeping me alive. When she kills me, I will become what she made Caleb. I want to writhe away from her grasp, but I can't move, can only stare up at her, too drained to even feel afraid.

Then her expression changes. Shock, surprise, anger; all seem to shimmer across the red eyes. "Get out of my way," she hisses.

"No." The answer is calm, steady, and oddly familiar. I blink, and when my eyes open, I see Cass, standing between Keziah and my fallen body. "You won't touch her."

This can't be Cass the vampire, who has been a stranger since the day she was turned, a fierce, savage creature who has slaughtered a path through the bayou with ruthless efficiency.

The voice I hear is Cass my friend, the gentle, steady voice that for months I've heard only in my memories, the girl who held out the hand of friendship on my first day at Deepwater High.

The girl my brother fell in love with.

"Cass?" I hear Connor say, his voice filled with so much uncertainty and hope that it pierces even the dull husk of my being, touches me within.

"I see you, Keziah," Cass says, her voice heavy and rich with pain. "You can't command me. Not with Harper's blood inside me. You won't even fight me—you're too worried about how strong I might be now." There is no triumph in her tone, just her words, stark and sad. "You're right to be worried. I *am* strong. Stronger than any of our kind, I think. And I won't allow you to take Harper.

"You should run, Keziah. Before I let the wolves take you. Let *Connor* take you." There's something, a particular emphasis, in the way she says Connor's name. It has a significance, I know, but through my fading awareness I can't think what it might be.

"You wouldn't," Keziah hisses, but there is a strange note beneath her rage that I know is fear. I open my mouth to draw breath, but with a suffocating horror, I realize I can't.

I'm dying.

The voices around me fade. The light of the world narrows, then falls away from me into a pinpoint, and I lack even the strength to cry beyond it.

"Harper!" I hear Connor's voice as if it comes from far away. I want to tell him I love him, that I will always love him, my beautiful brother who has been everything to me, who always will be my family, my heart. I feel love drawing me inward and onward, vaguely aware that it is all that truly matters, all that ever mattered.

"She's dying!" Connor roars in the distance. "Someone help me! Harper is dying!"

I wish I could tell my brother not to be afraid. I am here. I will always be here. I am both myself and beyond myself, and I know that life is nothing, just a pathway to another life, and I am already reaching for it.

"Get away from her!" An inhuman roar breaks through the fog. My brother is gone, and other arms are holding me, arms that tether me to this earth, even as I am beginning to float from it. A familiar, rough voice says: "Drink."

My mouth is forced open and something is falling inside me, a trickle that becomes a river. In my mind, it is like a river of golden sunlight tumbling in a joyous, life-giving rush onto the wasteland of my body. Like a desert after rain, it awakens every cell it touches, and that is how I see it in a strange internal movie, my body as desiccated ground that bursts suddenly into miraculous bloom. There are the flowers of my night garden, opening in a dark, passionate rush of color. The burnished depths of the river at twilight, fiery orange and spinning. A golden sun like spring after a long winter, radiating at the center of me. The deep green of the grass in the clearing, emerald and rich, and cradled within it, the crimson heart of the bayou rose, strong and vital. The sky above my internal garden is brilliant blue, glistening so bright at the edges it shimmers, and far in the distance an indigo infinity beckons, sustaining me in this life and beyond.

My eyes fly open as Antoine's wrist falls away from my mouth. "Take her," he says, speaking to someone I can't see. "Take her and go."

"No," I start to say, but Antoine is already turning away, and to my astonishment it is Tate who picks me up.

"You were dead," I whisper, but the words barely make a sound. He hears them anyway and smiles grimly.

"Not quite." He turns his head and Cass is there, her eyes wide and serious on my face. Then she glances behind her.

"Are you sure?" she says, and again I hear Antoine's voice, rough and hard as he answers.

"Yes. Go!"

Somewhere nearby, I hear Keziah scream, a hideous, furious thing; but it is too late for me to call out to Antoine, for Tate has picked me up and is running through the night, and I am flying, into nothingness, the river far below me and the sounds of battle falling behind.

CHAPTER 15

WATER

$\mathcal{I}$ have barely time to register our flight before we are home—but it is not the home I once knew. I am fundamentally changed, every particle of my being awakened by Antoine's blood.

The mansion feels both strange and familiar.

I wonder that I have never noticed the smooth richness of the floor under my bare feet, the way the scent of the river layers the air.

As soon as Tate puts me down, I go to the back of the mansion and open the French doors. I've always liked air movement through my living space, but now, as dawn draws near, I seem more attuned to the soft currents than ever before.

Nothing looks quite the same.

In the moonlight, the trees seem shrouded in a soft incandescence, a silver gleam similar to the Spanish moss hanging from the live oak in the driveway, but less substantial. The earth itself feels warm and alive, so joyous I want to sink my hands and feet into it and simply drink it in. I'm aware of buds on the trees yet to open, and the moonflowers tiring as they sense the approaching dawn. The mansion itself seems to wrap around me, sharing its secrets. I can see the great, old trees from which its original beams were cut, and know they live still, on the grounds. I feel birds stir in their branches.

Most of all, though, I feel water.

It is in the air caressing my face, tiny droplets like the finest mist. It runs through every blade of grass and leaf, a pulse I can feel, if not actually see. The river at the end of the slope feels unutterably powerful, slow-moving but inexorable, a tide that surges in my body and against the earth.

I'm so caught up in the myriad of sensations that I'm not entirely aware of Tate leading me gently into the kitchen, Cass making coffee. She hands me a cup and her hand touches mine. I almost recoil with shock. Cass's skin pulses with life. It feels smooth as satin, yet rich and warm, and almost without knowing what I'm doing, I grasp her hand, rubbing my thumb back and forth over her skin, fascinated by how thrilling it feels against my own.

"Harper." Cass's voice is hers again, nothing like the cold stranger I've become accustomed to. "Can you speak?"

"Yes." The word seems full of sensation inside my mouth. I wonder that I've never noticed the miracle of speech before, the thousand tiny vibrations inside that make sound. I can almost see the word hanging in the air, feel the tiny moisture droplets everywhere rearrange themselves to allow it to be heard.

"Are you okay?" Cass is looking at me concernedly. "I'm so sorry, Harper. I would never have drunk from you. It was Keziah—" her voice breaks off as I touch her face, marveling again at the supple strength of her preternatural skin over the being beneath.

"You're so beautiful." I smile at her. "It's no wonder Connor loves you so much."

Her face crumples and a single, gleaming tear tracks her perfect skin. "I made him become a wolf," she whispers. "And my mother, Harper . . . my mother is dead." She gives a harsh sob and spins away, standing at the kitchen door, grief rippling the air behind her. "I can feel everything," she whispers, her face turned away. "When I drank your blood, Harper, it was as if every mouthful gave me another memory, another piece of my soul, until the person I used to be slotted back into place inside me. The rest of me is still there. Noya, even Keziah. I can sense them inside me. But I'm *me* again." She turns back, her eyes soft and full of pain. "Will this last? Will I stay who I am now, or will it wear off? I don't want to be Keziah's creature, not ever again. I'd rather be dead," she says fiercely.

"I'm not sure anyone knows the answer to that." It's Tate who answers her, his voice quiet. "I'm not sure any of us really know what effect Harper's blood will have." He takes my hand in his own, studying my face curiously over the table. "How do you feel, Harper? You seem—different."

"I feel alive." I smile at them both. I'm so overwhelmed by sensation that it's difficult to speak. I touch Tate's face and his eyes flare in surprise, his eyes swiveling briefly to Cass. His skin feels extraordinary, too, though different from Cass's, cool and sleek, like the pelt of a leopard. I wonder that I've never before noticed the complexity in Tate's being. He wears the face of the Natchez man he once was, but I can see Antoine inside him, a fiery river of strength that glows behind his eyes. Deeper still I see the darkness of the French soldier, like iron that has been tempered in that fiery strength to become something both fine and invincible. "You carry so much inside you," I say wonderingly, feeling the layers under my hand. "I never realized who you were, before now."

"Harper," says Cass tentatively. "Are you still—yourself?"

"I think so." I tilt my head to one side, trying to feel the answer to her question. "I'm just . . . more." I smile, joy bubbling up inside me. "Where's Antoine?" I say, looking around. "And Connor?"

"We had to leave them." Tate glances at Cass then back to

me. "Antoine told us to get you out of there. We thought you were dying, Harper."

The joy is still there, but fear is at the edge of it now, like a black parasite on flowers. "I'm not dying. I'm fine. But Antoine can't fight Keziah alone."

"I didn't think he could, either. But it seems Antoine can still surprise me." Tate pulls something out of his pocket that gleams in the soft glow of the kerosene lantern when he puts it on the table.

"His ring," I breathe. I pick it up. The silver feels warm and alive to the touch. It gives me a faint shock to hold it. I can feel Antoine imbued in the metal, the remnant of his being inside it. Thin lines inside the ring catch my eye, and I turn the band in the light. Inside it is engraved the word *always*, repeated in both English and French: *always, toujours, always, toujours,* marking the metal in an unending pattern of eternity. Tears glisten in my eyes as I hold it, distorting Tate's face when I turn to him. "Where did you find it?"

"Antoine gave it to me. The last time I saw him, before I left for Haiti." I marvel that I hadn't noticed the ring was gone, in those first weeks when Antoine was still here and hadn't yet entirely lost himself to Keziah. But I had been so worried, I recall, that I was forever studying his face, his eyes, for some clue as to Keziah's presence in his soul.

"When he gave it to me," Tate goes on, "Antoine said that if he should lose himself again, find himself under Keziah's control, his ring was the one thing he thought might bring him back. Other than your blood, of course."

"Antoine knew about your blood?" Cass looks at me in mingled fascination and sorrow. "He knew how this feels, and yet he wouldn't drink from you himself?"

"He refused to." I roll the ring in my fingers, absorbed by how it feels. "Even when I begged him to."

"If he didn't drink," Cass says, "how did he resist Keziah?"

She shudders involuntarily. "You have no idea how it is, Harper, to be under her command. As if she's inside your skin, part of you. I don't know how anyone can defy that. How did he do it without your blood?"

It's Tate who answers. "Antoine's defied Keziah before. The first time was many years ago. Then he did it again, the night you were made, Cass." Tate nods at the ring in my hand. "But when he gave me this, he was more afraid than I've ever known him. I think he knew his ability to withstand her was waning. And he was right," he says grimly. "When I went to him, as he'd asked me to do, and showed him the ring, he didn't react. In fact, he did the opposite." He glances at me then looks away. "Antoine attacked me," he says in a low voice. "I barely escaped with my life. I thought him lost forever. All trace of the man I knew was gone."

"Keziah ordered him to kill you," Cass says.

"He said you were dead." I try to focus on speech. It's difficult. There is too much to feel, to inhale. "When Keziah asked him if you were dead, he said *it is done.*"

"He did leave me for dead." Tate frowns. "But he knows, too, that any such death could only be temporary. One drop of blood and I was restored. He must have known that would be the case. All I can think is that he left me for dead so he could answer her truthfully. He must have known she would ask, and he would be forced to answer. Leaving me dead, temporarily at least, was his way through that." He looks at me. "But he chose to save you," he says. "It wasn't the ring, Harper, or your blood. Antoine saw you being attacked and found a way to defy Keziah, to overcome her control. I don't know how he did that."

"We need to make sure he is okay." I'm suddenly restless, needing to feel Antoine beside me, craving him like a physical ache. Nothing else seems to matter other than having him close. "We need to go to help him."

The sound of the van pulling up outside interrupts me, and a moment later Callie bursts into the kitchen. She pushes Cass unceremoniously out of the way and kneels in front of me. "I thought you were dead," she says, in a quavering, fierce whisper. "Connor thought so too." She looks around the kitchen, frowning. "Connor's not here," she says, a statement rather than a question. "Jeremiah, either."

In a moment Cass is at Callie's side, her eyes flashing with a glimmer of her previous, savage self. "Is Connor in danger? Is he hurt? What did you see?"

"Cass," says Tate gently. "Let Callie go." Cass looks down at her hands gripping the girl's shoulders. With a visible effort she backs away. Callie, however, seems not at all intimidated.

"Something happened with the wolves," Callie says. "Right after you left with Harper. They began circling Antoine and Connor. I heard Connor say he had to go, that the wolves wouldn't let him fight. I didn't understand that. He ordered me to go, and then Jeremiah made me get into the van, and I thought he was coming too, but he didn't. And I'm not really sure how it happened, but somehow Connor drove the van onto the road, and then he leaped out and told me to keep going. He made me promise, Harper." Her face is a picture of guilt. "I didn't want to, I swear, but Connor was so sure, and I was scared for you; then I saw him change into a wolf as he ran toward the trees, and somehow I just kept driving, until I reached here."

"They're all alone." It's the first time since I woke up to this new life that something has penetrated the strange layer of golden beauty all around me. "Connor and Antoine are facing Keziah all alone."

"And Jeremiah," Callie adds. "Jeremiah is there."

"You have to go." I turn to Tate. "To help them. We can't just leave them there."

"I can't." Tate's voice is tight.

"What do you mean, you can't?" Tension rises in me like a tidal surge, a force I can actually feel.

"He commanded you." Cass is watching Tate. "Antoine commanded you to stay with Harper, didn't he?"

"But he's never done that," I say, turning to Tate. "You said that in three hundred years, Antoine has never commanded you."

"He never has." Tate gives me a half smile, a pained, twisted thing. "He summoned me once, and that, too, was to care for you. Tonight he summoned me again. To the clearing. After leaving me for dead, he summoned me. It was perhaps the only thing that could have dragged me from the fog I was in, forced me to find someone upon which to feed. Then, when I came to his side, he commanded me to take you—and to keep you safe. He ordered me away from the fight. I'm bound by his command, Harper. Bound to your side, until he releases me, or until he is killed. Antoine wanted to make certain you were safe."

"Then he's alive," I breathe. "If you're still bound, it means he's alive."

A charged silence is broken by Tate's phone ringing. He listens briefly for a moment, then hangs up.

"It was Avery. When Connor tried to fight at Antoine's side, the wolves rebelled. Remy's only chance of getting the pack under control was to order Connor back to this side of the river. Connor should be here shortly." Tate turns to Cass. "Connor said to stay here and wait. If you go back over the river, the wolves will kill you."

"But what about Antoine?" I say, looking between them. "And Keziah?"

"What about Jeremiah?" Callie is white-faced, her voice strained.

"Avery said that when she and Connor left the clearing," Tate says soberly, "the wolves had cornered Antoine and Keziah. They were getting close to attacking."

The tidal surge inside me becomes strong as the river. I leap to my feet. Callie and Cass fall away, startled. "Harper? What's happened to you?" Callie is staring at me in confusion, and I realize she doesn't know anything about what I've become now.

"I'm going." My voice seems to echo inside me and without. "I'm going over there. I won't let them die."

"No." Cass pushes me back into my chair, and even with my newfound sense of power, I'm no match for her strength. "I'll go."

"You can't resist her," I say, at the same time as Tate says, "It's too dangerous, Cass."

"I *can* resist her." Cass meets my eyes. "I have your blood inside me, Harper. All of it. You know the power I have. Nothing can stand against me. Not like this."

She touches my hand and I can feel it, the strength inside her, and I know it to be true.

"I can't let Antoine die for me." Her voice is sober. "I live because of him. He might not be my Maker, but he created me, put the sun in my body. We're joined. I won't let him die." She bends forward to whisper in my ear. "Tell Connor I had to go. Tell him I love him. Will you do that, Harper?"

She searches my face and I nod, knowing she has to go, just as I know that she does not think she will return, and I wish I could do something, say something, to stop her, even as I know it is already done.

Cass touches my cheek. It is sweet and fleeting, and I think that I will remember it forever, even as she flies through the mansion and down the slope, over the river, to the other side.

CHAPTER 16

WHOLE

Cass is barely gone when Connor's truck lurches to a halt, the door opening and closing before the engine has stopped turning. "Harper!" he calls from the porch, taking the steps in an audible leap. When he appears in the doorway, his face is gaunt and afraid in a way I can't recall ever seeing before. His eyes, bloodshot and exhausted, light on me and he lunges forward, pulling me to my feet. "Harper!" For perhaps only the second time I can remember in all our years together, Connor hugs me fiercely. "You're safe," he says, his voice cracking. "I thought you were dead. I honestly thought I'd lost you, Harper."

I can feel the wild beat of his blood, the savage wolf in him electric against my skin. As with Tate and Cass, I see Connor in a different way than before. I feel the conflict in his soul, the twin lives he leads, the pull of the wolf and the heart of the man, entwined and vital but tearing him apart. Amid them I feel love. And fear.

That is the light and dark that lives in us all, I think abstractedly as I stand in my brother's embrace. *In everyone I feel that conflict, expressed in different ways. Fear. And love.*

105

"I'm fine, Connor." I step back, holding his hands. "I'm not hurt."

His eyes narrow slightly as he looks at me. "But you're changed."

"Yes." I don't look away, and I don't deny it. "I am."

"How?"

"I don't understand yet. But it's okay, Connor. I'm okay."

The wolf part of him hears and understands, but the man in him looks around, frowning. "Where is Cass?"

Tate stands up, glancing at me. "Cass left, Connor. She went back over the river."

What color is left drains from Connor's face. "I told Avery to tell her not to go. Remy has lost control of the wolves. If they so much as catch Cass's scent, she'll be dead."

"She knows the risks." Tate's face is grave. "Cass is strong, Connor. Full of Harper's blood. She may not be so vulnerable as you think."

But Connor is shaking his head. "She can't stand against Keziah and the wolves," he says shortly. "Not without Antoine." Then he glances at me guiltily, and I try not to react.

"You don't know Antoine is dead." I'm proud of how steady my voice is.

Connor holds my eyes but doesn't answer.

"What about Jeremiah?" Callie holds up her phone. "I've called him a dozen times. He's not picking up. And he's the only one over there without supernatural powers."

"I don't know, Callie." I think it's the first time I've heard Connor use her name or address her directly without any hint of anger in his voice. "I didn't see Jeremiah. I'm sorry."

He turns back to Tate. "What did Cass say? How was she?"

Between us, Tate and I try to explain what's happened to Cass. "She's herself again," I say eventually. "I'm not certain for how long, and neither is she. But for now, she's stronger even than Keziah."

Connor's face is dark. "You don't understand the power Keziah has over her," he says. "You think you do, because of Antoine, but it's far, far worse for Cass. Keziah has a hold on her that is so strong it's like a physical bind, a chain that pulls her this way and that." I remember seeing Cass sway toward Keziah back in the clearing.

"I think that pull is gone now," I say slowly. "I can feel the change in her."

Connor's eyes narrow. "What do you mean, you can feel it?"

I look between him and Tate. "People look different to me now." I put my hand on Connor's. "Like now. I can feel you. Connor, my brother. The man you are. But I can also feel the wolf inside you." *And something else*, I want to say. *I can feel the reason you have been so angry at me all this time.* But that is not my secret to tell, and so I don't. "I can see the wolf in your eyes," I go on. "I know how it feels to run across the ground silently, to feel the power in your muscles, like an itch trying to break through your skin from the inside, an energy so strong that at first you didn't know whether to kill or run or tear your own body apart. The restlessness. The animal inside you that is always instinctual now, reacting sometimes before your mind can logically recognize what is happening."

Connor stares at me. "You can feel all that," he says flatly.

"Feel it. See it, too. In—colors. Textures." I shrug. "I can't explain it, not really. It's like I can read the air and feel what is inside it, what forms are made of."

"Then you know how I feel right now?" His face is hard.

"I know everything inside you wants to fly across the river and stand at Cass's side. I know that so much as the thought of losing her makes your world black and unbearable."

"Then you understand that I have to go." He starts to back away.

"No, Connor." I shake my head. "You can't go, and Cass doesn't want you to."

"I *can* go, and you can't stop me."

"If you go to that side of the river, you could die, Connor. If not at the hands of Keziah, then by the wolves themselves." My words stop him at the door.

"Is that something you can see, as well?" He says tightly.

"In a fashion. I can't explain it. But the earth is different on that side of the river, Connor. It isn't yours, over there. You aren't the same as the other wolves. Your wolf is bound to this ground, where the potion that created you was made. Your wolf is bound to Antoine."

"And it's bound to you," Tate says, watching me. I nod reluctantly.

"Yes, to me." I go to Connor and put my hands on his shoulders. He shivers slightly. "You feel it," I say. "I know you do. We're linked, you and I." I won't say it for him, but I know he understands it. "Here, we are safe. Keziah can't fight you or me here. But there—on the bayou side, Connor, we're not so able to fight her."

"And Cass is?" He stares at me, his face tortured. "How can Cass fight her? She was made here too, by Antoine and Noya, with Keziah's blood. How can she survive over there?"

"I don't know that she can." I'm still holding his shoulders. "But I do know that you can't, Connor. Or at least, not with your full power. If you go there you will be at risk. Cass didn't want that. It's why she left before you got here. We have to trust her, Connor. At least give her a chance."

"Harper." Something in Tate's voice makes both Connor and me turn to him. He's looking around, frowning. "Callie—where did she go?"

As he speaks, we all hear the van start up. "Callie!" I race for the door, but the van is hurtling down the driveway, through the gateposts before even Tate is outside. "Go after her," I say to him, and his hands clench in frustration.

"I can't," he says through gritted teeth. "I'm bound, Harper."

"I'll go." Connor is already pulling off his T-shirt.

"Go!" He is already leaping off the porch. "But if she makes the bridge, Connor—"

"I know," he calls over his shoulder. "I won't cross it." Then he leaps into the shadows, a black streak in the darkness.

Tate and I sit in the silent kitchen. The night is growing deeper, moving into the occult hours where time no longer seems to exist. Sensation is coursing through me, almost as overpowering as the emotions gripping my heart.

"Antoine has fought Keziah before," Tate says quietly.

"Not like this. He gave me his blood, Tate. A lot of his blood. He's weak, and she's had him under her control for weeks now." I turn the silver wedding band slowly in my fingers. *Always. Toujours.*

"It still brought him back, Harper. The ring. Antoine came back to himself because of you. Whether it was when he saw you attacked, or before that, some part of himself was still conscious, still survived in there. Antoine is stronger than you think. Stronger than any of us know, I suspect."

"I don't know," I whisper. "I felt her, Tate. The cold death of her blood. I can't imagine how it would be to have been created with that."

He looks at me curiously. "And now? Can you feel her still?"

"No." I realize it's true. "There's no trace of her left inside me," I say. "Whatever Antoine has made me, what I am now is stronger than her blood. I don't think she is sure what I have become. I suspect she's never fully understood it. I think that's why she didn't turn me earlier, why she watched and waited for a while."

"You told Connor you can see people differently now."

"I can see so much. Feel so much. It's as if before the world was a painting. Now, it's a movie in technicolor. One with different dimensions and special effects. I don't understand it yet, not really."

We both leap to our feet at the sound of someone approaching, but when Connor enters the kitchen, one look at his gloomy face is enough to make us sink down again.

"Callie made the bridge before I could catch her." To my surprise, Connor slumps down on the floor, his arms on his knees, head hung down dejectedly.

"She went back for Jeremiah," he says, in a muffled voice.

"They're friends," I say gently. "Callie cares about him."

"She didn't even ask for my help."

I don't want to say the obvious—that nothing Connor has done would have given Callie the idea he would want to help.

"I let her down." Connor's voice cracks as it did earlier on Cass's name. "She's my own blood, and I let her down, just as I let you down. And Jeremiah, he's over there with nothing to protect him. He stayed because of Antoine. And I left them to face Keziah." He slumps further, his fists clenched in frustration. "I don't even know who I am anymore," he says brokenly. "I've been so angry, for so long. After I took the potion, when I felt—" his voice breaks off, his eyes sliding away from mine.

"When you felt my blood," I say gently.

He looks up sharply, his eyes narrowing.

"I didn't mean to put my blood in your potion, Connor." I shake my head. "I cut my finger on the knife. The blood was on the wolfsbane. I didn't know it would affect you, change you. I would never have done it if I'd known, I swear to you."

His eyes search my own, seeking the truth, and when he finds it, he nods slowly. "I think I knew that," he says quietly. "Deep down. But knowing it was your blood that did all this, that even linked Cass and me . . . it felt like I had no control over anything anymore."

"You think it's me that links you and Cass?" I frown. "Surely you know that isn't true."

"Isn't it?" Laughing harshly, Connor passes a hand over his face. "It's the force that binds us, Harper. We can both feel it. It's why Keziah is so afraid of me. And it's also why Cass hated you so much. And now she's full of your blood, and we'll never know if it's real or something else."

"That isn't true." We both turn around at the sound of Tate's voice. He's watching us from the door, his face grave. "Whatever Harper's blood contains, it isn't enough to forge that kind of bond in a vampire. You forget: we are immortal, made of different stuff than you or anyone else. What we feel comes from a different place than human emotion. It is bound in us, immovable and unassailable. It's the reason we find our Maker's bond so hard to overcome. It is forged in emotion. The only way we can overcome it is if what we feel is forged in a stronger emotion, one great and enduring enough to remake that hard core of ourselves." He smiles in a sad way. "I can tell you from experience that it is very hard to find that kind of emotion. In fact, the only person I have ever known to do so is Antoine. And even he has struggled." He meets Connor's eyes. "Harper's blood works on Cass *because* of what she feels for you, Connor. It isn't the reason she feels it."

Conflicting emotions shift across Connor's face. "You don't know that," he whispers hoarsely.

I touch his face. "But I do." His eyes meet mine, searching for the truth there. "I can feel what is inside Cass in the same way I can you, Connor. And please believe me—it isn't my blood that binds her to you. She loves you, Connor. As much as you love her. It is the force that makes her what she is. And you—you became a wolf because of her, Connor. Because you love her. My blood is nothing compared to that."

His hand comes up, covers my own. "It is, though," he says roughly. "Your blood is the reason I didn't die that night, Harper. I felt it, the moment it hit my cells. It wasn't the potion that brought me back to life. It was you. You—and Tessa—" Tears fill his eyes and his voice shakes. "I could feel her, hear her whispering to me. It was both of you who called me back to life.

And then tonight, when I saw you on the ground, Harper, I thought I'd lost you both, forever. I'm so sorry—I'm sorry for it all—"

And then I'm on the ground with him, and a little while later I hear Tate slip from the room, leaving my brother and me together, broken but somehow, mercifully, more whole than we've been in a long, long time.

CHAPTER 17

ACTIVATED

The night slips by as we sit in the silent mansion, waiting. We've had no word from anyone.

Worn out from emotion, we don't say much. Connor, now showered and dressed in old jeans he'd left behind, sits on the front porch steps, coffee left to go cold beside him.

Tate remains in the kitchen, still and silent.

I sit out on the back steps, staring through the night to the river. It isn't that I can see through the darkness, but rather that the darkness has a texture I can see between. It is one of the thousand tiny distinctions I find myself trying to process while also trying not to think about what is happening across the river. I can feel myself transforming, my body altering in some fundamental way, but I can't find the words to describe it and I feel strangely self-protective, unable to withstand scrutiny or questions.

My mind returns to Antoine, Cass, Callie, and Jeremiah, surrounded by wolves determined to kill them, and Keziah, who will do everything in her power to regain control over her two children. It didn't go unnoticed by me earlier that she referred to Tate as Antoine's *progeny*, while she herself spoke of Cass and

Antoine as her *children*. It's typical of Keziah's narcissism, I think, that she finds it impossible to imagine anyone else capable of creating or feeling a bond as deep as that which binds others to her.

That in turn makes me think of what Tate said about vampires and emotions, the bond between him and Antoine. I already knew the Maker's bond is one felt by the made vampire, a tie that is based on emotion and thus able to be manipulated by the Maker. Even I know there is nothing more powerful than our emotions. To take our deepest vulnerabilities and make them into a weapon, to be deployed by the Maker at will, seems unutterably cruel to me. I remember Tate telling me once that the bond between him and Antoine is based on the love of brothers, as they had considered themselves before Antoine's transformation. Tate said he could not stop feeling that love for Antoine, no matter how cruel Antoine had been to him in the intervening centuries, and despite the fact that until recently, Antoine had never invoked the bond between them.

I've never directly asked Antoine why that was. Now, though, I wish I had. I wish I'd asked him many things. More than anything, I wish I'd found a way to make him activate me before this whole night began. The one thing I feel certain of, with every cell his blood touches inside me, is that the being I am becoming could never be defeated by something as dead and cold as Keziah. I'm stronger than her. I can feel it. I just wish I could use it.

Blackness has shifted to the subtle texture of predawn, and mist curls above the slow- moving river when the white van returns.

The three of us race to the doors, pulling them open before Jeremiah has cut the engine.

"Callie," he says hoarsely. A silent, pale Connor is already pulling Callie's limp figure from the van, carrying her inside. Jeremiah's face is drawn with exhaustion, and he holds his arm at an awkward angle, but he waves me off impatiently when I ask if he is hurt. He stumbles as we mount the stairs and follow Connor as he lowers Callie on to an old sofa. She has such a mercurial, lively presence that I've never truly noticed how slender she is. Lying on the large sofa, eyelids so pale they are almost translucent, her collar bones sharp beneath her skin, she seems terribly vulnerable.

"She's not dead." Connor's voice is heavy with relief.

"What happened?" Tate asks, kneeling beside her.

"She needs your blood, Tate," Jeremiah answers. "She was—drunk from. Not by Keziah," he adds, when Tate frowns. "But please hurry. She's been unconscious since I took her from the river."

"What about Cass?" says Connor roughly, as Tate bites his arm and lowers it to Callie's mouth.

"Cass will be fine," says Jeremiah briefly, but there's a hard note in his voice and he turns away, looking back at Callie. "Will she be okay?" he asks anxiously.

"She's lost a lot of blood." Tate gives Jeremiah a small smile, wincing slightly as Callie's hands suddenly come up to his arm, pulling it toward her with surprising force, though her eyes remain closed. "It will take a little time, but she's strong. She'll recover." He lets her drink a little longer then gently unclasps her fingers and removes his arm.

I put a hand on Jeremiah's tense shoulder, shivering at the contact. It will take me a while, I suspect, to become used to the way people feel to me now, as if when I touch them part of them comes out to meet me, traveling under my skin and into my awareness. "Remember Avery," I say. "It took a while for her to recover after Keziah attacked her, and Antoine fed her his blood." Jeremiah glances at me and I know he is remembering, too. The tension goes from his shoulders, and he slumps back on the ground, hands on his knees as Connor's had been earlier, staring at Callie's prone figure.

"The wolves were fighting both Antoine and Keziah," says Jeremiah dully, before any of us prompt him. "Antoine was trying to knock them away, to stop Keziah from killing them. But the wolves seemed insane, out of control."

"Remy lost control of them," Connor says, slightly defensively. "It's not their fault. Keziah is the very thing they're born to destroy, even more than normal vampires, I think. You don't know how it feels when she's close—like poison under our skin. It's hard for Remy to keep his head, let alone the others."

"Was it hard for you?" Tate asks, looking at Connor.

"Not as hard," Connor says, glancing sideways at me. "I'm not—made the same as them. I find her easier to resist." He prompts Jeremiah. "Go on."

"The wolves were in a frenzy. For a long time, it was just snarling teeth and claws. I wanted to help, but everything moved so fast." He looks at me almost apologetically.

"You wouldn't have had a chance," says Connor curtly. "You would have only been in danger."

Jeremiah nods reluctantly. "Then Remy came. Antoine was on one side of the clearing, Keziah the other. They had wolves behind them, between them, circling them—preventing them from escaping. Remy ran between them, trying to get the wolves under control, but it wasn't working, and Keziah and Antoine couldn't move. For a while, it was a stalemate. Keziah was trying to call Antoine," he says, looking at me. "He was resisting her, but I could see he was weakening. The wolves were still circling, and he was struggling to fight them off. Keziah was getting closer." His voice shakes slightly. I can see the naked fear in his eyes at the retelling, feel how it must have been to watch someone as strong as Antoine, Jeremiah's only family, facing such impossible odds. I'm holding on to my own sanity by clinging to the knowledge that if Antoine were dead, Tate would know. He would feel it. As long is Antoine is alive, we have a chance.

"Go on," Connor says tightly, and I realize my brother is desperately trying not to ask about Cass, just as I am about Antoine. I take Connor's hand and squeeze it. After a moment, he returns the pressure.

"Remy started to get the pack under control," Jeremiah says. "But by then, Antoine was weak. One of the wolves managed to bite him."

Dread clutches my chest. A wolf bite is fatal to vampires, can only be cured by blood from the same wolf, while in wolf form. Something tells me that in their current state of mind, that option isn't likely.

"Keziah was coming for him," Jeremiah says. "Antoine yelled at Remy to get the wolves out of there. I think Remy understood that no matter what they thought before, the wolves couldn't defeat Keziah alone, that Antoine was the only thing standing between them and her." Jeremiah shakes his head. "She's so strong," he says, a kind of wonder in his voice. "Even the whole pack, working together, couldn't get near her."

"That's because she drank their blood." Tate's voice interrupts us, and we all turn to him. "The night Keziah escaped from the cellar, she drained all the bayou men, down by the river. It was Antoine's blood that brought them back to life—and activated them in the process. When Keziah drank from them, she took their power into her own blood. She made what they are part of herself." His face is dark. "I should have seen it before. The wolves can't kill Keziah. She already owns what power they have." He meets Connor's eyes. "It's also why she was so afraid of you."

Connor swears under his breath, a vicious curse quite unlike the brother I know. "We could never understand it," he says bitterly. "The wolves could run as fast as her. Could track her. They've even taken down other vampires before." Seeing our looks of surprise, Connor's mouth twists slightly. "They pass by, from time to time. They don't pass the bayou, though," he says.

"But Keziah avoided us. No matter how close we got, we could never bring her down—even if we could get Caleb."

"I think Antoine realized that." Jeremiah is holding Callie's hand. He looks tired and defeated. "When he told Remy to go, there was something in his voice that must have penetrated, because a second later, the wolves were gone." He falls silent, and I want to beg him to hurry up, but I know that whatever he is struggling to say won't be helped by my pushing him. "Antoine had fallen," he says, not looking at us. "I started to run over to him, but Keziah threw me out of the way. I hit a tree and for a moment I was knocked out, I think."

That explains the hurt arm and the scratches.

"When I woke up, Keziah was drinking from Antoine. I tried to get up, to go to them, but I couldn't move. It was like my whole body was just frozen." Jeremiah looks at me apologetically. "I don't know what Keziah did to me, but I felt like I'd been compelled, even with the frankincense I have in my system. I'm sure it was her that did it. And Keziah wasn't just drinking from Antoine, Harper. She was draining him. I know, because he looked just like you did, when Cass—" His eyes dart to Connor, and he subsides.

"Go on," I say, my voice sounding oddly high even to me.

"She took every last drop of blood from him. I saw it." Jeremiah shudders.

"What does he mean?" I ask Tate. "Every last drop? How is that possible?"

"It's the surest way to weaken a vampire completely," says Tate. "But it is also the most repulsive, revolting act imaginable. We don't drink from one another. Sometimes, perhaps, to sustain, to give life to another, if it is absolutely necessary. But to deliberately drain another—" His entire body recoils. "It's a vile act. One of torture and subjugation. Keziah did it because she knew he was too strong for her to control. Draining him, replacing his blood with her own, was the only way to make Antoine her slave again."

"Her own blood?" Fear grips me at the idea of that dark, insidious poison wending its way through Antoine's beautiful, sun-filled body. "No. Please tell me he didn't drink from her," I say to Jeremiah, hearing the desperate note in my voice and unable to stop it.

"No." Jeremiah glances at Connor. "That was when Callie and Cass arrived."

"Callie and Cass arrived together?" Connor asks.

"I don't know if it was intentional or not," Jeremiah says. "But Keziah saw Cass coming at her. She dropped Antoine to the ground and stood up to face her. Cass looked—different. Strong. But Keziah looked different, too."

"Keziah was full of Antoine's blood," says Tate tightly, and I can see how it hurts him. "She would have been twice as strong as ever before."

"When Keziah faced Cass," Jeremiah said, "Callie attacked Keziah from behind."

"Callie?" Connor and I stare at each other in shock.

"Callie attacked Keziah?" my brother asks. "How?"

Jeremiah looks down at Callie's hand sleeping in his own, and for the first time since his return, he smiles. "She was incredible," he says proudly. "That sword she trains with—she's so fast with it! She thrust it into Keziah from behind, right through her heart, then whipped around to the front and cut her throat. When Keziah turned on her, Cass attacked, and Callie got out of the way. Cass had Keziah, too," says Jeremiah, and for a moment his eyes gleam. "They had her," he says again, looking at Callie.

"So what happened?" Connor can't hide his impatience.

"Antoine," says Jeremiah quietly. "Antoine was dying."

"But he's a vampire," Connor says dismissively.

Jeremiah shakes his head. "It was different. Callie was trying to feed him her blood. He wasn't responding."

"It's the wolf bite." I remember the night on the mound, when Antoine wouldn't respond. "The poison. If Keziah took all his blood, and if the wolf venom can't hurt her—".

"We don't know that," Tate interjects. "It may be able to hurt her. Though perhaps not in diluted form, through Antoine's blood."

Jeremiah continues the story. "Callie called out to Cass. She said Antoine was dying, that he wouldn't drink. Cass turned to Callie, let her attention slip for a moment—and Keziah ran away."

"Even after a sword through her heart," Connor says flatly, "and having her throat cut." He shakes his head. "Go on."

"By that time, I was with Callie. We both tried to feed Antoine our blood. He wasn't responding." Jeremiah's face pales. "I've never seen him like that," he says quietly. "Not even that night he made Cass. He was so still—" his voice breaks off. A moment later, he takes a deep breath, and goes on: "Cass didn't hesitate, though. She opened up her own wrist and fed him her blood."

"I thought you said you never did that?" Connor says to Tate.

"Cass wasn't feeding him her blood," I say slowly. They all turn to look at me. "She was feeding him mine." There's a short silence while everybody follows this line of thought. "Cass drained me," I say. "When she did, it cut her bond with Keziah. That's what Cass was doing. Trying to break the bond between Antoine and Keziah. And she knew my blood was the only thing strong enough to counteract the wolf poison."

"Your blood can heal wolf venom?" Connor raises his eyebrows incredulously. "Are you certain of that?"

"Perhaps not heal completely," I say. "But neutralize—yes, I think so." I look at Jeremiah. "Did it work?"

"In a fashion." Jeremiah glances at me and Connor, as if reluctant to say anything more.

"Jeremiah." I'm getting frustrated. "Just tell us what happened."

Jeremiah tilts his head. "Fine," he says, in a you-asked-for-it kind of tone. "Antoine drank. He drank so much he almost drained Cass; he couldn't stop himself. Then, when he finally pulled away, Cass was so weak she could barely move—so Callie fed her." He gestures at the prone figure. "Cass had a little trouble stopping," he says grimly, glaring at Connor. "So Antoine pulled her away, and ordered me to bring Callie here. I think that just about brings everyone up to speed."

CHAPTER 18

ARMORED

*I*n the charged silence that follows his story, color chases across Connor's face, from hectic red to white and back again. He stares at Callie's prone figure on the sofa, and I watch the emotions shift behind his eyes. The first light of dawn is a golden thread on the horizon, but the day is not here yet, the air still and hushed. It's so quiet I can hear Callie's shallow breathing, feel Jeremiah's pain and anger. When Tate shifts, I'm instantly alert. His eyes meet mine.

"They're here," he says quietly.

He doesn't need to say who is here. I can feel them, Cass and Antoine, feel my blood inside them reaching for me, like mercury joining inside a thermometer. I feel them pause outside the mansion. If I close my eyes, I can envisage exactly where they are, at the base of the stairs, hesitating.

"They're unsure what kind of reception they will receive." As I say that, Callie's eyelids flutter, and she sits up abruptly, startled. "Cass and Antoine," she says, staring at Jeremiah. "What happened to them? Did it work?"

Jeremiah slumps against the sofa, his mouth working. "You can ask them yourself," he mutters. "They can hear us."

A moment later, the two figures appear at the door. I feel rather than see them. I'm almost scared to face Antoine. Every cell of my body thrills with his blood, and his nearness heightens the sensation, so it's almost unbearable.

"Callie," says Cass, her voice trembling. "I'm so sorry. I didn't mean to hurt you."

"You didn't." Callie dismisses her concern with her customary sharpness, sounding so like herself I almost smile. "You needed it. And besides: you saved Antoine." Her eyes shift to look over my head; Antoine is right behind me. "Did it fix you? Harper's blood? After the wolf bite?"

"We went to the pack to make sure." Antoine's voice is deep and smooth, vibrating inside me with such power I tremble slightly. "Remy gave us the blood from the wolf that bit me. But we couldn't have done it without you, Callie. None of it." Her small face colors with pleasure, but Callie doesn't say anything, just curls into the sofa. Her hand, I notice, is still held in Jeremiah's.

"Keziah?" Connor is looking at Cass, and I know he's not asking only about Keziah's whereabouts.

"Neither of us are controlled by her now," says Cass. "Even after Antoine drank from me, whatever Harper's blood did is permanent, I think. It changed me, in some fundamental way. I can feel Keziah. But she can't control me."

I am so aware of Antoine behind me that it's hard to focus on what they're saying, particularly when, a moment later, he says my name. "Harper. Can I speak with you?"

I don't answer, just turn, leaving the room without looking at him or anyone else. I move through the mansion to the slope at the back and down, out of human earshot at least, to where the water garden lies silent and waiting in the hushed moment of time before daybreak.

"Harper." I feel him behind me, but he doesn't touch me. "I understand if you find it difficult to trust me. If you don't want to hear me. But I needed to tell you I'm sorry anyway. No matter how inadequate an apology may be, after everything that's happened." I'm barely listening to his words, though. I can hear what is behind them, feel what is inside him, and so instead of answering him, I say, "You need my blood."

"What?" His voice is blank with shock.

But I know it already, can feel it inside him, the conflict. "You need my blood," I say again.

"No." His voice is tight with frustration. "I can still hear Keziah. But I *can* fight her, Harper. I've done it before. And what Cass gave me is enough to put a barrier in place."

"But it isn't the same." I say what I know he can't. I force myself to turn, to face him. The gold in his eyes is dull, as if the life has been drawn from it, and there is a faded texture to his skin, like fruit that has begun to dry in the bowl. It hurts me to look at him. I can feel the withered agony inside him. "My blood is different now," I say quietly. "Changed. I am not what I was when you activated me. I am—more, now."

"I can feel that." He steps closer. I can barely breathe. "You glow," he says softly. "Inside. It's like a hidden light that shines from every pore of your skin. You're so beautiful, Harper, I barely trust myself to touch you."

"Because of you." I step toward him and hear his sharp intake of breath, see the darkening in his eyes. "I told you once before to take my blood." I'm determined that he will hear me. "If you'd only listened to me then, taken me, activated me before Keziah took control, all of this could have been avoided. I won't allow that to happen again, Antoine. I've just got my brother back. Cass. Callie almost lost her life tonight." His face closes over, but I don't care. "You don't know how strong I am now," I breathe. He's so close I can taste him on the air. It's intoxicating. "No vampire has drunk from me as I am now," I say. "I don't think they could, Antoine, and survive. Only you. It was you who activated me. You live inside me." I put one hand on his chest and he trembles at the shock of it. "You feel it," I whisper. "You feel what I am now. I want to live inside you, like you do in me. You made me, Antoine. Let me give this to you. Let me make you as strong as I am, make you something Keziah can never take from me again."

His hand covers mine, sending shockwaves into my body. "What if I can't stop?" he says roughly. "You don't know, Harper. You have no idea how potent your blood is. I can feel it, under your skin."

"You will," I whisper, stepping closer so only a heartbeat separates us. "I know you will." I tilt my head, so my neck is exposed to the thin thread of a golden dawn. I feel the groan deep in his chest. He gathers my hair in one great hand and holds it beneath my head. I can feel the longing in every fiber of his being. "If I hurt you," he rasps, "call for Tate, Harper. For Cass. Don't let me hurt you—"

"You won't." It is me who pulls his head down to my neck, my body aching for him now, something inside me reaching for him, desiring this more than anything, as if my blood is already yearning to find its way back to the source that activated it. "Take me," I whisper so softly I don't know if I say it or think it, my arms twining about his neck as his arm comes beneath me and lifts me effortlessly against him.

Then his mouth is on my neck, and the world slips away.

This! I think exultantly. It is everything I remember and more, so much more. I feel his shock as my blood hits his system, the viselike tightening of his arm around me, pulling me into him with such effortless power I'm helpless in it, my only thought to surrender to the dark thrill of the flow between us. My entire body seems to sing as he claims it, flowing toward him rather than being taken, the essence of me recognizing its alchemical partner, seeking to fill what is missing inside him and being nurtured in turn. With every ounce of me that passes into him, something else bursts into life inside me. I writhe against him, my hands curling into his skin with longing. When he pulls his head away from me, eyes blazing in his face, I reach toward him, trying to bring him back to me.

"I can't, Harper," he gasps. "I have to stop. I have to, or I never will." He throws his head back, holding me against him with one arm beneath me, the other hand cradling my face. "It feels like nothing I've ever known," he says wonderingly, and when he looks at me, I see the sun blazing deep inside him. The withered color is gone, his skin glowing bronze and supple once more, bursting with life. "Keziah is gone, Harper. Every part of me is armored against her. I can feel it. She can't penetrate this. And you." He shakes his head, tracing my lips with his thumb. "What *are* you?" He stares at me. "It's as if life itself is inside you. Every part of you is alive, shimmering. I can feel it inside me."

"And you inside me." My lips move against his hand. "It's as if you feed me, when you take my blood. I feel more alive, not less. There aren't the words . . ." I want to kiss him, am so drawn toward him I can't resist—then I find myself put down, Antoine a short distance away, smiling wryly, his eyes smoldering.

"If we start," he says, "we won't stop. Not now. The way I feel right now, maybe not ever. I think we should go back inside first, make sure everyone is safe."

I try to draw a steady breath. I know he's right.

"Later."

His eyes deepen and darken. "Later."

CHAPTER 19

GARETH

*A*ntoine and Tate disappear shortly after our return to the house. I suspect it is not only what Tate discovered in Haiti that he wishes to talk about. The bond between them is deep and old, and there is still a lot that lies unsaid between them. The fact that Antoine has, for the second time, used his power as a Maker to command Tate seems to suggest a breaking of the ice I thought him incapable of, and that gives me a warm feeling inside.

It isn't easy to reenter the company of others. The changes in me are so deep, so profound, so ever-changing, that being around anyone feels unbearably sensitive. I am aware of every breath, every word, every emotion.

"I know what it's like." I'm in the kitchen when Cass enters. I heard her coming, but I spin around anyway when she speaks. Her voice sounds like she is right next to me, though when I turn, she is in the hallway. She half smiles. "It's the same for new vampires. Well, not the same, exactly. Your blood has a different kind of awareness. As if you can bend space, see through it somehow. It's like having a coating of gold or silver on the inside."

"*Armored*. That's what Antoine called it."

"Exactly. Like armor plating." Cass smiles tentatively. "The heightened awareness, though, the feeling that everything is *more*, somehow—that is similar to what a vampire feels, at first. It's why I found it so hard to be around you all. I could hear the blood moving inside you. Feel it. Taste it, almost. Having you near me was like waving the most delicious food imaginable in front of a starving person. Particularly you, Harper." Her smile becomes a little rueful. "I was both fascinated and repelled by you. And Keziah . . . she wanted you so much it was like a burning thirst inside her that I could feel. But she was afraid of you, too. I could feel that as well, particularly after I had your blood inside me. She didn't know what drinking from you would do to her. I think she was frightened even to give you her blood—she couldn't tell what would happen."

"How do you feel now?" I ask her. "Now that you're free of her?"

"It's strange," Cass says slowly. A painful cloud shadows the clear lines of her face. "It's hard to remember everything that happened. The people I killed. My mother's death." Her voice quavers on the last words. "Keziah killed my mother, Harper. I watched her do it. I can never take that back. I can never see my mother again. I don't know how anyone lives with that. Not . . . forever." Her eyes are deep pools of sadness. "For the rest of eternity, I will know that my mother is dead because of me. I never got to tell her what an amazing mother she was. She never saw grandchildren. She never even saw me graduate, and she worked so hard to make sure I did, Harper. She was so proud of me." Her voice has faded to a painful whisper. "I can never undo that wrong."

"Cass." I move across the room and hold her hand, feeling the now-familiar rush as her skin touches mine. "You saved my life. You saved Antoine's life. Because of you, Keziah is running now, probably unable to harm any of us, ever again. You are a good person. You always were. And if we're playing the blame game, it begins with me, as you once said." I meet her eyes. "I should have told you Keziah was under the house. I should have told Connor. What you are, Cass, everything that's happened—it's my fault. All of it. I can never take that back, either. My brother is a wolf because of me."

"Maybe we should stop looking for someone to blame," she says softly.

I nod. "I think perhaps we need each other more now than we ever have. Avery, too." Cass shakes her head at that, sorrow darkening her face again.

"Avery's angry. She's been angry at me for a long time." She swallows and looks away. "Wolves are dead because of me," she says in a pained voice. "I've killed more than one of them, Harper. Avery and Remy can't forgive that. They can't forgive me for the people from the bayou who died at my hands. I don't blame them. I can't forgive myself, either."

"What will happen to the wolves now?"

"They aren't at peace." It's Connor who answers, coming quietly into the hallway behind Cass. "I've spoken to Remy on the phone, but I suspect it's the last time I will. He's a good man, but he's under pressure. Many of the wolves had problems long before they turned. Drugs, mental health issues. Now for months, they've been forced to track a quarry they can't actually kill. Stand by while another one kills their own with impunity. They're angry—and dangerous. There are also more of them than there were."

"More?" I let go of Cass's hands and face him, surprised. "How?"

"We're not sure. Remy's mom, Lori, thinks it might be a result of the sudden activation of so many at once. Younger people in their community are turning, those who have Natchez blood, no matter how far back. It seems to be happening at adolescence, and when vampires are nearby. Five in the past month alone."

"More wolves," I breathe. That can't be good.

"They'll stay on their side of the river," Connor says.

"For now."

"Yes." He meets my eyes. "For now."

Callie and Jeremiah appear behind him. We move into the kitchen and spill onto the front porch, Connor lounging against the doorway with a shadow of his old smile, Cass cuddled into his side, Jeremiah and Callie out front.

"How are you feeling?" I ask Callie through the open window.

"I'm good." She gives me a half smile. "You know. For being half-eaten by a vamp and all." I hand her a mug of coffee and a sandwich that she tucks into eagerly. Callie looks up and catches sight of Cass's pained expression. "Joke," she says, around a mouthful of sandwich. "Don' take it personal." She looks at Jeremiah. "I'm gonna have to teach you how to fight. Properly. You nearly got yourself killed tonight."

"Sure." Jeremiah seems entirely unperturbed by her insults. "After you get some rest."

Callie rolls her eyes. "I'm just fine." Her eyes rest on Connor and her light manner fades. "Probably not sticking 'round, anyhow," she mutters, taking another bite of her sandwich. Connor and Cass exchange a look. Connor lets go of Cass and walks over to Callie, nodding at Jeremiah, who moves aside.

"Callie," says Connor gently. "I'm sorry for how I've been since you came here. I should never have treated you that way."

"Don' bother me none." Callie's Memphis accent is thicker than I've ever heard it, her eyes downcast and resentful. "Never asked you for nothin'. Don' need nothin' from you, neither. Gonna stay with Jeremiah for a while, ain't that right, Jem?"

Jeremiah casts me an apologetic look. "I think Connor's trying to say that you're welcome to stay here."

"Never stayed nowhere I ain't welcome. Ain't startin' now." Callie gives Connor a mutinous look. "Your daddy was mean, too. He tol' me to get on the next bus. Right after he asked me if I had any cash." She shakes her head dismissively. "Anyhow. Don' matter, like I said."

"Callie." Connor leans forward, his hands clasped between his knees. "I know this probably won't make much sense. But Gareth—our father—he never told me about you. Never even mentioned that he'd met someone, let alone that he'd had another child."

"So?" Callie folds her arms and stares at him.

"So, it hurt, I guess." Color stains Connor's face. "When he was with your mom, he wasn't with me. I woke up one morning and Gareth was just gone. No warning. Not even a note. I wasn't even ten." He glances at me. "It was before he met Harper's mom. By the time a neighbor realized I was alone, there was nothing in the house left to eat, and the power had been switched off."

"Sounds familiar." Callie's face hasn't softened, but some of the accent has left her voice.

Connor nods. "The neighbor said I could stay a few weeks, but I knew that eventually she'd call Social. Every day, I expected to see them parked out front when I came home from school. Then I got in one day, and Gareth was sitting at the table, all cleaned up, sober. Said he'd met someone new, and he'd come to get me."

"Mom," I say. Connor nods. "I don't know what happened, how he got clean, but I was so happy I didn't ask questions. You don't when you're young. Then I got to your house." He looks at me, and I don't see the man who is part wolf now, who I've found so hard to reach these past months. I see instead the skinny boy I remember hanging back at the edge of the lawn on a sunny Baton Rouge day. I hear Tessa say, in her little girl's voice, *You want to play with us?* And I remember the look on his face, half hopeful, half terrified, as he came slowly over and sat on the grass beside us, pretending to actually like playing with our stupid dolls. "It was the only time in my life I could remember having a real home," he says quietly. "Then barely two years later, Gareth fell off the wagon again."

"And you stayed with her family," Callie says, the resentful note back in her voice.

"Not at first. I went with him. But he left me again—and again." Connor's never told me this, never said what happened in those months he left our home. "Finally, I realized he wasn't coming back, and he wasn't changing. That's when I went to Harper's mom and asked if I could stay."

"Least you had somewhere to go."

"I know that. But, Callie—" Connor meets her eyes. "When I met you, all I could think of was Gareth leaving. I'd always known he had somewhere else to go. I guess I just hadn't realized he had another child, as well." He shrugs. "It hurt, is all."

"You think Gareth left you for us? For *me?*" Callie almost laughs aloud. "I didn't even know my father's name 'til after my momma died. If he ever came 'round, I sure don't remember it. As for him coming back to you all cleaned up? Well, that's the only part I do know." She looks at Connor. "Whenever I asked her about my father, the only thing my momma would ever say was that he'd stolen the one chance she'd had to get clean. She said they'd done one big deal, with the idea of using the money for rehab. They were both going to get clean. But he lit out with the money. Left her broke. She realized he never even intended to stay. Then she found out she had a baby on the way." She shrugs. "She never had a nice thing to say 'bout him, so I learned not to ask."

"I'm sorry, Callie." Connor puts a hand on her arm, and she doesn't pull away. "I really am," he says quietly. "For everything he did to you." He glances at Jeremiah. "I understand if you don't want to stay here, after everything that happened. And it's true that Cass and I will also be here now, on and off at least, and I'd understand if you don't feel safe with us around. But I do want you to know it's your home. For as long as you need it. You're family, Callie. I know I didn't get that right the first time, and I sure as hell wish you hadn't had Gareth's sorry ass for a daddy. But if you'll let me, I'd like to try to make it up to you." He looks at me. "We both would."

Callie watches him the whole time he talks, her blue eyes beady and hard, scrutinizing his every word. When he stops talking, she studies him for a long moment. "What happens if you go dark again?" she says abruptly. "I've lived with addicts, like I said. Seems to me this wolf thing, vampire thing too, ain't so different from that. How do I know you won't turn on me when you've had enough?" She nods at Cass. "Or that she won't suddenly get thirsty?"

"You don't, I guess." Cass smiles gently at her. "Even I don't know that. I wish I did. But Harper's here. And from what I saw in the clearing, you're no mean fighter. I'd say you know how to take care of yourself."

"So we gonna stay here together? Like some weird-assed Brady Bunch?"

"Well, it's big enough," Connor says. "I can't hear Harper's awful music from my end of the house, even when she plays it loud. We might also go back to Cass's mother's house. We haven't decided yet. In the meantime, I'm going to renovate the old slave quarters in the west field. Cass and I might stay there for a while. "

"Really?" I've barely been over to the tumbledown ruins on the other side of the tree line. "I didn't know you were working on those."

"I've got two rooms finished already. Enough for us. For now, at least."

"So that's why not much has been done on the mansion."

He shrugs. "I was finding it hard to come in here. But work helps clear my mind, so I did that instead."

"Slave quarters." Jeremiah raises his eyebrows as he looks at Cass. "That isn't weird for you?"

"Actually, I find it rather empowering," says Cass primly. "There's a certain satisfaction to be had in owning a place in which one's ancestors were held captive. And I think a little distance is healthy." She looks at me as she says this, and I color faintly at the sly smile on her face.

"So it's settled then," Connor says, not least, I suspect, to cover his embarrassment at Cass's comment. "You'll stay."

"Okay, then." Callie nods. "But I don't want y'all telling me what to do," she says, giving us a rather threatening look. "I'm used to running my own thing. Don't need no parent figures telling me how."

"Cross my heart." Connor grins.

"An' I don't cook."

"You should fit right in." Connor smiles at her and gets up. He meets my eyes. "Okay?" he says quietly.

I nod, feeling happiness sing through my veins. "Okay," I say, and for the first time since Keziah escaped, I feel like it is.

CHAPTER 20

LILIES

*I*t's dusk when Antoine returns.

Callie is with Jeremiah at the river house, as inseparable as ever. There is nothing more than friendship between them on the surface, but I sense a deeper current running between them that is yet hidden from sight, perhaps even from themselves. It is one of those things I know is better kept to myself. It is a strange thing, this ability to sense the unknown. It will take time for me to learn how to navigate the unseen pathways of thought and feeling.

Connor and Cass have gone to her mother's house, for tonight, at least. It will take them some time to pack up her things, for Cass to mourn what has been lost. I suspect mundane tasks are welcome to them both at the moment. When Antoine's truck pulls in, I'm sitting on the back porch, looking down at the water garden.

The water lilies are still hiding beneath the surface of the pond. Summer is almost fully upon us, and I can sense they will open soon. The magnolia trees are rich with flower, a blaze of fragrant white and red. The garden seems to hum with life, making my blood rush and skin tingle, seeming to call me with a dark, heady compulsion. Tonight feels special. After coming so close to death, I feel a certain decadence, so earlier I opened one of the boxes marked FANCY in my room and chose an indigo silk slip dress that feels cool and soft on my skin.

The air changes, becomes dense and exciting. It's Antoine coming toward me. I don't turn, just watch the slow, treacle river and feel the quiet intoxication of his nearness.

"It has been the longest day of a long life." His voice is low and intimate and seems to reach into my soul. "The feeling of you inside me, Harper— it's unlike anything I've known. I feel every ray of sunlight, every particle of air on my skin. I feel both human and something entirely *other*." I shiver as his hand touches my neck, trailing sparks down my shoulder. His nearness is electric. "Tate told me that in the Taíno tradition, you are the embodiment of Abatey. Neither of us are entirely certain what that might mean, for now at least. Tate will continue to research."

"Cass says she feels completely protected from Keziah, yet she drank from me before I was activated." It's something that's been bothering me, but it's hard to focus. I'm distracted by the lazy movement of his hand on my skin, his thumb at the nape of my neck. "But you say my blood is different now."

"Cass drained you, Harper." His voice roughens on the word, and I feel the sudden tension in his hand. "It's a different thing from taking blood. She took the very core of you inside herself. That affects us even when it is only a human we kill. Sometimes we carry a shadow of the person for days, weeks, even. It's one of the reasons we tend to drink without killing. To take a little blood—that doesn't touch us. But when we drain a person completely, it leaves an imprint. I think that your nature means the shadow is a permanent one, something even more powerful than the creatures we are. Something so alive that it changes us in some fundamental way."

"I think that having my entire body drained," I say slowly,

"meant that when you fed me your own, it had a more dramatic effect than it might have otherwise."

His thumb stops moving on my neck, and he moves around so he can see my face. "It felt like a river," I say, remembering, "flowing onto a dried land. It was as if you brought me to life. I could see it, see the garden of my own body. Everywhere the river touched burst into life. A new life, a different kind than before." I shake my head, frustrated at my inability to properly describe what I mean. "I know what Tate said about me being the embodiment of Abatey. But I think your blood made me something different, Antoine."

"Something like what?" His eyes search my face. "Do you crave blood?"

"No, nothing like that." I feel color flood my face. "I crave you," I whisper. "It's like your body is part of mine, and mine part of yours. All day, it's as if I've known where you are, can feel you moving through the air. And when you touch me—"

"It's the only time you feel whole," he finishes. His eyes are dark, without end.

"Yes."

"For me, too." He takes my hand and leads me down the stairs. The grass feels rich and warm underfoot, the air heady with the scent of the river mingled with that of my nightgarden. "I don't remember being human," he says, as we walk down the slope toward the jetty. "Sometimes I've caught glimpses of it when I've drunk from people over the years. After I drank from you the first time, felt my body regenerating, I thought perhaps that was what it was like to be human. I wondered that I wouldn't remember something so exquisite."

"This isn't being human." I curl my hand in his, thrilling at the touch of his skin. "I was human yesterday. It didn't feel like this."

"No." He stops by the night garden, beneath two magnolias that reach out to almost touch one another. The first summer blooms are already falling from the branches, petals soft and fragrant lying fresh on the ground. "I know that now," Antoine says, catching a petal as it falls, holding it between his thumb and forefinger. "You are more than human. What is inside me—Harper, every part of me is alive. It won't last, I know. It can't last forever. But for now, it's like the power of the earth itself trickles through my body, my soul. Everything in me is alive—and craving you." He trails the magnolia petal down my face, my neck. I tremble, my lips parting, and when I look at him, his eyes are cobalt and gold, deep with desire. "All day I've pictured you like this," he says in a low voice. "Here, by the night garden. I've felt as if you were drawing me back to you."

"I felt drawn, too," I whisper, as his lips push the straps of my dress from my shoulder, and the magnolia petal drifts lower, trailing soft fire over my skin. "As if the garden was waiting for us. Both of us."

"And now we're here." His lips move on my skin, slipping the dress from my body so it falls in a midnight pool atop the flowers. I gasp at his mouth on my belly, his large hands laying me down on the petals. My hand curls inside his shirt and he shrugs it off, his hard, sun-bronzed body gleaming in the final red glow of dusk. His hands cradle my face, and I reach up to cover them with my own, feeling the hard silver band of his wedding ring. His eyes search my face. "It brought me back," he says hoarsely. "The ring, Harper. It brought me out of the darkness, shone a light when there was none. Tate showed it to me, and suddenly it seemed like I could smell magnolias, hear you whisper my name."

"Always." I trace the band. "I didn't know you'd engraved it on the inside."

"It's on yours, too." He smiles through the growing darkness, and it seems to me that he glows, though the moon is not yet risen. "Before I ever gave you that ring, I knew what it was with you. I knew this was always." My body surges toward his and he takes my mouth. "But I didn't know this, Harper," he murmurs against my lips. "I didn't know anything could be like this is, with you."

I move suddenly and now it is him beneath me, the night air touching my skin as my hair tumbles down my back, and I arch against him, petals falling softly about us. "You're so beautiful," he says roughly, and then the moon is rising, and neither of us speak any words of sense for a long time.

In the velvet midnight I wake, turning in Antoine's arms so the night garden is laid out before me. The moon is high overhead, beaming down on the pond. The moonflowers are open, the night jasmine perfume on the air. Two bayou roses I haven't seen before bloom, crimson and rich, leading down to the water garden.

My eyes follow them. In the sheltered water, two green tips appear beneath the still surface.

Slowly the green shoots rise above the water, leaves tightly furled, as if the flowers hidden within are secrets only I can see.

*D*ear Tessa,

I'm writing this in the early hours, when the world is still and Antoine is gone, hunting.

I think I dreamed of this once.

Happiness.

But I never knew it could feel like this. I wish you were here, to feel it with me. I wish I could explain how it feels. And above all else, I wish I knew it was forever.

I'm changed. Everything is changed. I'm the person I always was, but . . . I'm different, too. More, somehow. And I'm not sure what that will mean as time goes on. I don't think things can stay the same. I'm not sure I want them to. But I don't know what's coming, either. I can feel something is, something big. I just don't know what it is.

Keziah is still out there. I guess this change could have to do with her. I don't feel so afraid of her now, though. I don't think Keziah can hurt me. When I think of her, I feel a surge of power. I might not know exactly how to fight her. But I feel like I could.

Tonight the summer sky is low and heady, the clouds rolling

up along the river, lit from behind with electrical flashes. The air is still, charged, crackling with the coming storm. I can smell rain in the air, feel the leaves and flowers already opening exultantly in anticipation.

The world feels rich and alive, so full of sensation it is almost overpowering. Perhaps I would feel this way even if I were in a city apartment, but I don't think so. I think I belong here, in the Mississippi river silt, amid slow-moving water and heady skies. I think I was born for this earth, in this time. I was meant to be here. With Antoine. With everyone this life has brought.

The only person missing is you, Tessa. You are a hole in my heart that no time can take away. A part of me that will forever be missing. There is so much I wish I'd said to you before you died. I know you needed me to bid you goodbye, to understand that you had to go, couldn't stay. But I couldn't do that. I held on to you until the final minute, willing you to live—when all you wanted was for me to say goodbye. I wasn't what you needed me to be in those final moments and, oh, Tessa, I wish I could have been that for you. Since the changes in my body, I understand far more about what others need. What you needed. I know what I should have been for you, back then, what I should have said. And even though I know it doesn't matter now, still, I wish I could go back there and do that for you.

You were always what I needed, Tessa. Even now, you are what I need. If I felt you before, now I am filled with you. You live in the air and the flowers, in the earth all around me.

What I would give to tell you my secret.

But I can't. Not yet.

Soon though, Tessa.

Soon.

· · ·

Your twin,
  Harper

Turn over to read sample chapters of Dusky Dahlia, the next in series, or buy it on Amazon to keep reading.

PROLOGUE

ear Tessa,

The moon is high over the water, and the world is asleep. Antoine is gone, hunting as he often does in the early hours when he knows it won't disturb me. I'm glad he isn't here. I woke from a dream so startling it still feels real, and I'm writing to you because you are the only person I can trust with it.

Lately, it seems I hear you on the wind, in the water, more than ever before. Sometimes when my hands are in the earth or the breeze moves, I hear your laugh, so soft it is there and gone by the time I've turned to find you. I see your face in the billowing cloud over the river in the late afternoon. The birds chatter in your voice, and there are days I'm so certain you are beside me that I begin to speak before I realize it's only my imagination.

I thought the longing for you would grow less with years, not greater. I feel old, Tessa, like I've lived a hundred lifetimes instead of barely a quarter of one. When I see our friends preparing for college, their world feels a universe removed from mine. There are no surprises in their choices. Jeremiah and

Avery are both going to Ole Miss in Oxford, Jeremiah studying history, Avery pre-med. Cass, sadly, isn't going to college at all. I know she was planning to study music. After everything that has happened, though, she doesn't really trust herself near humans. And I don't think she likes being away from Connor. They're living in her mom's old house. If Avery has spent the summer being brittle and distant with me, Cass is simply sad. Connor told me not to ask about it, so I haven't.

Callie has spent much of the summer with Jeremiah. I think she will miss him a lot when he goes.

They all seem so distant from me and the odd life I lead. Yours has become the most real voice in my world, Tessa, as strange as that might sound. Which is why you're the only person in whom I can confide the truth about my dream last night.

In my dream it was also late at night. I was sitting on a rock by a vast, still sea. Moonlight rippled across the surface. All about me was silent emptiness, just the moon and me amid the indigo night, the water still as glass. Gradually I became aware of something drawing me forward, across the water, to where the moonbeam reflection was most brilliant. I traveled across the water as if carried on the moonbeam itself, an intense rush of energy pulling me to where it shone the brightest. The light grew stronger, until a brilliant blaze drenched every cell of my body, overwhelming my every sense until the light was all there was. Below me the still water began to churn. For the longest time, I was held in that euphoric blaze of light, suspended over a wild sea, surrounded and filled by a force stronger than any I've ever felt. Then, as suddenly as it had come, the light was gone, the moon returned to a pale disk in the sky, the sea quiet. I found myself back on the rock, staring out at the still, glassy surface, as undisturbed as it had been before I was drawn to its center.

I woke a moment after that.

I'm writing it down before I forget, though I suspect I will remember every moment of that dream for the rest of my life.

It's been six weeks since the night Antoine drank from me. I knew there was something special about that night. Something unlike the other times we'd been together, something beyond us both, that seemed to draw us to one another with the inevitability of magnets, made us lose ourselves in a melding of soul and body unlike any force I've either known or imagined.

When I woke after my dream last night, I knew what that something was.

I'm pregnant, Tessa.

No matter how impossible or improbable, that's the truth. It's what I felt in the dream and know in my body.

I'm pregnant. Even saying it sounds insane.

And if it sounds that way to me—how on earth am I going to tell anyone else?

Your twin,
Harper

DUSKY DAHLIA SAMPLE CHAPTER 1

TEST

There's nothing simple about buying a pregnancy test in a small town.

The main drugstore in Deepwater Hollow is owned by Avery's parents. I've barely seen Avery for weeks, and I suspect Mr. and Mrs. Fairweather aren't my greatest fans. They already blame me for Avery's relationship with Remy. Avery's parents worked hard to send themselves to college, then returned to make something of themselves in a town that always looked down on them. They have high aspirations for Avery that definitely don't include a tattooed man from the bayou with a dubious past. Somehow I doubt buying a pregnancy test is likely to improve my standing with them.

I go to the drugstore on a day when I know they usually work out back and have an assistant on the desk. When the bell on the door jangles to announce my presence, however, it is Avery I find behind the counter. My heart sinks. I can't exactly turn around and leave again, so I plaster a smile on my face and grab some random hand cream from the shelf on my way to the counter. I haven't seen Avery for weeks. I'm struck by how sad she looks, her usually glossy hair dull and in a messy braid, her face pale.

"Hey," I say tentatively.

"Hey." She gives me a small smile as she rings up the hand cream. I try not to look at the row of pregnancy test boxes on the shelf nearby. "I'm sorry I haven't called." She stares down at the counter, fiddling with the cream, something clearly on her mind.

"Avery?" She looks up, and the realization that she is fighting back tears pushes my own dilemma momentarily to the back of my mind. "What's wrong?"

She glances over her shoulder to where her parents are watching us beadily through the glass window. "Remy and I broke up." The watchful faces of her parents and the way she whispers it gives me a fair idea of what might be the cause of the breakup.

"Was it because of your parents?"

Avery shrugs. "Them. And other things." She glances up as if she wants to say more, but then shakes her head and dashes away a stray tear. "Anyhow, I'm off to the University of Mississippi soon. And everyone knows long-distance relationships don't work." Her smile is barely a ghost.

I don't blame her for not wanting to talk about it. I know better than anyone the world of secrets we share. It's not for me to judge those kept by others. I cover her hand briefly with my own.

"I'm so sorry, Avery." I mean it. I know she loves Remy, and I'm pretty sure he never got over his luck in landing someone as gorgeous and smart as Avery. I'm sad for them both. "At least you'll have a friend at college. Jeremiah is going to Ole Miss as well."

"He is?" Avery's face lights up. "What's he studying?"

"History." I smile wryly. "Turns out Tate coming to Deepwater High was the best thing that could have happened to Jeremiah. He's spent most of the summer glued to Tate's side, reading books I can't even lift, they're so heavy. He's currently obsessed with the French Revolution, and he's super excited because Ramon, an old friend of Tate's who saw the whole Napoleonic era live and in technicolor, is coming to visit." When Avery looks confused, I hold up my hands. "Don't ask me. History wasn't my subject either. But I guess one bonus with immortal friends is having prime source material on hand. Jeremiah and Callie are ridiculously excited about meeting Ramon. It helps that Callie speaks French and Spanish. She taught herself, apparently." I shake my head. I sometimes suspect Callie is hiding an entirely different person under her gangster image. The first day she began speaking to Antoine in passable French, we both stared at her in open-mouthed astonishment, but Callie just shrugged and said she'd picked it up from a Cajun boyfriend her mother had when she was a kid. Spanish she'd learned from the Mexican kids at her boxing club. "I like the way languages work," she told us, leaving Antoine and I speechless. I realize that Avery, however, doesn't seem quite so impressed.

"So that skinny kid is still hanging around Jeremiah," she sniffs.

"Callie has been a good friend to Jeremiah." Whereas Avery, I can't help but think, has been all too willing to exploit Jeremiah's almost slavish devotion when it suits her, only to discard him without a thought when something better comes along. Avery, though, true to form, is oblivious to my subtle rebuke.

"I'll call Jeremiah when I get off work." She's already looking more like her old self. "It will be good to have at least one friend at college." She glances at the hand cream. "Have you been gardening too much again?"

"Occupational hazard," I lie, forcing a smile. "Connor and I are getting a greenhouse set up so I can start a nursery."

"So you're really going to just stay here, in Deepwater? With

—him?" She doesn't need to say Antoine's name. I can see the mixed emotions on her face, feel the envy, guilt, and curiosity wash through her. It's one of the many things I've become accustomed to over the summer, this immediate understanding of what others are feeling. It's not always comfortable. Sometimes I react to what I know people feel, rather than what they say. It's made for some uncomfortable interactions at times. It took me a while to understand that people don't always want to be understood. So I choose my words carefully now.

"I've never wanted to go to college, Avery. You know that. All I've ever wanted to do is paint and grow things. I'm happy doing that right where I am. And yes, for now at least, Antoine and I are together." I pick up my hand cream. "But I guess we all know things change."

"Sure." She gives me a forced smile. "Well, I'll come see y'all before I go." She pauses. "Have you seen much of Cass?"

"Not a whole lot." I'm careful with what I say. "She's had to make a lot of adjustments, I guess."

"Haven't we all," Avery mutters, unable to keep a note of resentment from her tone. I'm guessing she still holds Cass responsible for Connor turning into a wolf and causing problems for Remy in leading the bayou pack. It's a drama I can't do anything about, and anyhow, I've more pressing matters on my mind—like where else I can buy a pregnancy test in a town where everyone seems to notice everything.

I'm saved from an awkward exit by someone else needing to be served, and I slip from the drugstore with a little wave. There's another, smaller drugstore on Second St. I'd avoided it because it's close to Witch Way, the shop once run by Cass's mom. I thought Cass would close it after her mom's terrible death at Keziah's hands, but she hasn't. I think it's given her something to do while she's working out what her life is going to be. Given that it will be an immortal life, I guess it's no small question.

Sure enough, just as I'm getting out of my Mustang in front of the drugstore, Cass comes out of Witch Way. I force a smile.

"I've just seen Avery," I say by way of greeting. "She and Remy have split up, it seems."

"Oh, no!" Cass looks genuinely sympathetic, though I know for a fact Avery has barely returned her calls this summer. Cass is just kind, even now, after living with Keziah's blood in her veins and months of her mind control. "Do you know why?"

"She mentioned college and long distance." I realize my mistake instantly. Cass turns away abruptly, but not before I see how her face closes over and feel the wave of frustration and loneliness inside her. "I'm sorry, Cass," I say quietly. "That was insensitive."

"It isn't your fault." Cass gives me a false, bright smile that I know better than to question. "As Connor says, in time I'll be able to study whatever I want. Just not quite yet." I nod, figuring silence is the only diplomatic response to that. For all her kindness, Cass is still a vampire and a savage one at that. I know she struggles with urges that Antoine says can take years, if not decades, to settle. At least in the shop she can walk away or close the door. A lecture hall, I guess, isn't quite so simple.

"Anyway. Did you come just to say hi?"

"Yes," I lie, with a bright smile of my own. "Just checking in."

"I'm fine, Harper. Really. You don't all need to check on me every second." Cass's eyes flash, and I get a momentary glimpse of the killer within. I nod again and step back.

"Sure," I say gently. "I'll see you round, Cass." She doesn't answer, but I suspect that's more because she doesn't want me to see her cry than because she's actually mad at me. I get back into the Mustang silently and give the drugstore a rueful glance.

In the end, I drive an hour to the next town to buy the test.

At a roadside gas station, I go into the bathroom and stare at the little white stick. I'd always thought it would take a long time for the results to appear.

It doesn't.

In a matter of seconds, I'm staring at two, unmistakably bright pink lines.

The test tells me what I already know—and what I equally know to be impossible.

I'm pregnant.

I drive home slowly, wonder and terror churning inside me.

SEEDLINGS

Antoine calls as I pull into the driveway. "I'm going to be late. The engine on the boat failed. It's going to take a while to fix." I can hear Jeremiah laughing in the background.

"You're on the river," I say, smiling.

"We'll be on the river a while yet," Jeremiah calls.

"He seems to be enjoying this."

"Oh, he is." Antoine's tone is light. "He's taking great delight in reminding me that engines don't care whether I'm immortal or not." I can picture Antoine as he speaks, eyes caught in the last rays of the sun, hair tousled by the river air. I feel a sudden, visceral tug of longing.

"Come home soon."

His tone drops a notch, sending a tremor down my spine. "I will."

"Oh, stop it," says Jeremiah impatiently in the background. "She'll still be there when you get home." I hang up to the sound of their banter, smiling to myself. Over a long summer in which nothing was more constant than uncertainty, Jeremiah's obvious delight in Tate and Antoine's company has been a source of joy. He's spent his days working with Connor on the mansion and his evenings pouring over history books with Tate, Antoine, and Callie. I've never seen someone so enamored of his college reading list. I'd never realized how much he loved history, but I suspect he hadn't either, until the arrival of both Tate and Callie, who between them seem to have brought his passion to the surface.

"You seem deep in thought." I spin around to find Connor behind me. The day is fading, and my brother has appeared as silently as the dusk shadows. I smile without looking directly at him and nod instead at the steel structure on the empty land beside the mansion. "The greenhouse is coming along."

"It's going to be all you asked for, I hope." Connor looks at it in satisfaction. "And you've already made a good start on the seedlings." He nods at the neat rows of pots by the night garden. He casts me a sideways glance. "But I get the feeling it isn't plants you're thinking about."

"Would you do me a favor?" I hand him my phone. "Would you take a photo of me, right now, here in the garden?"

"Sure." Connor looks at me quizzically as I pose. "Any particular reason?"

"I just want to remember this moment." I smile into the camera. "When everything is still at the beginning." My hand sneaks unconsciously down to my belly. I pull it away before Connor can notice.

"I'd say it's a lot further along than the beginning," Connor says. My heart almost stops, but when I look up he is smiling, and I realize he was talking about the garden rather than my belly. I take a shaky breath and keep smiling as he takes a few photos of me there. When he's done, I look at the smiling figure on the screen, marveling that it isn't completely obvious to everyone that I am different, that I carry a life within me now.

"I saw Cass today," I say, not least to distract myself from my thoughts. "She's not doing so well, with everyone heading off to college."

Connor's smile fades. "No," he says shortly. "She isn't." His smile is as forced as Cass's was earlier today. "Well." He turns back toward the mansion. "I'll leave you to it." I watch him walk away, the long, graceful lope that has become his natural gait since he transformed into a wolf. My brother is still my brother, but I never forget that, like all of us it seems, he is also so much more now. I know his inability to help Cass is frustrating and worrying for him. But he doesn't share that part of his life with me anymore. He and Cass are a unit now, as tightly bound as Antoine and I are. There are things only they share. I understand it and respect their privacy, but Connor is my brother, and it hurts to see him so obviously in pain, just as it does to see Cass's misery.

In the silence following his departure, I try to think of how I am going to tell Antoine that I'm pregnant.

He will say it's impossible.

I already know this. I've thought of almost nothing else since I woke from that dream. I can almost hear his arguments. Perhaps that's why I asked Connor to take the photo of me in the garden. I want a record of this moment, the brief pause when I can be alone with the miracle inside me before chaos erupts, which it surely will when I break the news.

My hand steals down to cover my belly again. I know I'm being fanciful, but it genuinely seems as if I can feel the life within me, just as I can when I plant a seed deep in the earth. It's a certain warmth, an inner density, the sensation of energy and matter gathering within. That blazing light that flooded my body. *That was you, little one,* I think, holding my belly in wonder. *That was you coming to me, from wherever it is souls arrive. From God, I guess.* I recognize the irony of thinking of God when I'm talking about a baby conceived by a vampire and Abatey incarnate. *An immortal killer and the modern embodiment of an ancient deity.* I shake my head. *What manner of miracle does such a union create?*

That thought should scare me, I know. But it doesn't, or at least, not for long. Some other inner certainty settles over me every time I touch my belly or think of the little pink lines on the test. It's too wondrous a miracle for me to feel afraid. I guess I can only hope Antoine feels the same.

I will tell him tonight, I decide. When he gets home. It's only been one day, but I feel as if I've been hugging the knowledge to myself for an eternity. I've had my private moment to come to terms with it. Now I want to share it with Antoine, no matter how shocked I know he will be.

The soft fragrance of red magnolia touches my face. "I wish you were here, Tessa," I whisper, an ache catching in my throat. "I wish I could share this miracle with you. I wish my little one could know you."

I'm here.

Her voice is so real I swing around, startled, then half smile at my own fancy. "It seems so real sometimes." I touch the petals of the magnolia. "Here, in the garden. As if you were in the soil, on the breeze. You told me that, Tessa." My eyes fill with tears as I remember that last day in the hospital, before Tessa ceased speaking. "You said I'd always find you on the breeze, in the flowers. You told me to put some of your ashes in my garden, so you'd always be with me. I couldn't even hear you at the time." I'm crying now, scalding hot tears I can't seem to control. "But I did what you asked, Tessa. I put you in the earth here. And I do feel you. Every day, with every breeze. Sometimes I feel you so strongly I would swear your hand is on mine, that you're standing right by me. I miss you so damned much, Tessa."

Night has fallen, and I draw a shuddering breath. I'm shaken by the sudden rush of emotion. I look around self-consciously, relieved nobody witnessed my little meltdown. *I guess it's hormones.* Don't they say that pregnant women are completely overly emotional? Just the thought feels overwhelming. I'm struggling not to cry again.

I'm going to need to get a grip.

I realize with a grimace that Connor's truck is still parked outside the mansion; I don't really feel up to his scrutiny. Then I realize Tate's vehicle is there as well and, as I take that in, Antoine's boat glides to a halt at the jetty below, and he leaps from it as Jeremiah tosses him the rope.

Great, I think resignedly. *Just what I need—a roomful of people with supernatural senses of observation.*

But for once, Antoine's attention isn't entirely focused on me as he strides to my side and kisses me in an unusually perfunctory manner. "Is Tate here yet?"

"I think so." I look up at his face, see the slate-gray eyes soften as his arms tighten around me briefly. "I thought you were going to be late," I say, my arms around his neck. He pulls me closer briefly and kisses me again, in a way that makes my breath hitch.

"I was. But then Tate called. It seems we have a visitor, so I had to deprive Jeremiah of the joy of watching me pretend to struggle with the engine." Despite his levity, there is a shadow behind his eyes.

"Ramon is here already?" Last I knew, Tate's friend was due to arrive in a week or so.

"Not Ramon." We walk toward the mansion, Antoine's arm still holding me close to his side. "Someone else."

I guess my secret is going to need to wait a while longer.

AFTERWORD

Buy Dusky Dahlia in the Amazon store to keep reading.

If you enjoyed Bayou Rose, please consider leaving a review on Goodreads and/or Amazon. Reviews help sell books, and I can't tell you how much I appreciate them!You can read Antoine's story, a prequel to the Nightgarden Saga, here. It is free and exclusive to readers!

Follow me on tiktok @paulaconstant.

Listen to the playlist that accompanies the Nightgarden Saga on Spotify.

You can also join the Nightgarden Readers Facebook group, and chat with others (and me) about the series.

If you'd like to be the first to read new Lucy Holden work, why don't you join my advance reader team? You can sign up on my website at www.paulaconstant.com/the-nightgarden-saga.com.

Above all, thank you. Do not hesitate to write to me and let me know any of your thoughts. I love hearing them.

Kindest regards, and all my thanks
Lucy Holden (Paula Constant)